EFFEL

EFFEL

A McDRAGON TALE – BOOK 2

PAM G HOWARD

Matador
9 Priory Business Park,
Wistow Road, Kibworth Beauchamp,
Leicestershire. LE8 0RX
Tel: 0116 279 2299
Email: books@troubador.co.uk
Web: www.troubador.co.uk/matador
Twitter: @matadorbooks

ISBN 978 1788037 549

British Library Cataloguing in Publication Data.
A catalogue record for this book is available from the British Library.

Printed and bound by CPI Group (UK) Ltd, Croydon, CR0 4YY
Typeset in 11pt Minion Pro by Troubador Publishing Ltd, Leicester, UK

Matador is an imprint of Troubador Publishing Ltd

MIX
Paper from
responsible sources
FSC
www.fsc.org   FSC® C013604

For my three young dragons, Charlotte, Grace and Chloe

BOOKS BY PAM G HOWARD

The McDragon series
McDragon
Effel

Mr Spangle series
Spangle

CHAPTER ONE

The rope tightened and the dragon roared in frustration, snorting angrily out of his nostrils – he couldn't move – he was trapped. He knew he was going to need the help of the young boy Petersmith again, because he was the honey in the trap and if the other dragons tried to rescue him they would be caught too.

* * *

The rain pattering on the tent was a soothing sound and, what's more, for a short time Peter had the space to himself. A school camping trip to Scotland was not his idea of fun at all, there were seven of them sleeping in the tent and it felt overcrowded.

Now where on earth was Spit's dragon scale? He needed to use it to talk to the little dragon before anyone came back. The last message he'd had from Spit was that there was something badly wrong – McDragon was missing. He had not been for his usual visit for a few days. Peter desperately wanted to know if there was any news at all but he needed his dragon friend's scale to do that. On his recent visit to the Isle of Harris, the young dragon Spit, had given him a scale from his chest so that they could use it to talk to one another. He had another dragon scale, which the adult dragon, Seraphina, had given him for the same purpose, but it was hidden at home for safe keeping while he was away.

He was positive that he'd secreted the scale in his soap box and that had been inside his washing kit but it wasn't there! He tipped the whole bag out carefully on top of his camp bed and went through each item individually. Nothing. The only reason he'd put it there was that he'd had to go out for the rafting trip on the loch and he didn't want to take any chances of losing it in the water.

He was beginning to panic!

Was McDragon alright? He really needed to know!

Now where on earth was that scale!

After searching thoroughly yet again he realised it was definitely missing, which was a disaster.

A head poked through the tent flap, "Peter, you need to come out for supper now!"

"I'll be right with you," he replied starting to carefully put everything back into the wash bag and checking it all over yet again as he did. He took another look over the sleeping bag and then inside it, in case it had fallen out unnoticed. Finally, he woefully had to admit defeat and give up before someone else came along to insist he came out for dinner.

Dinner today was cottage pie and baked beans which was quite filling and tasty and then there was a pudding. Each tent had to take turns at cooking and fortunately his tent's team had done their shift yesterday so they had tonight off.

* * *

The next day's role call was bright and early and the sun was beginning to shine through some misty light rain so a beautiful rainbow lit up some of the sky.

Peter thought to himself, "There is often a crock of gold at the end of a rainbow so where does that one end?" and he pinpointed where he thought it should be. Strangely the end of it seemed to move over to the left a tad as he stared at it.

"I'll go there when we have our break and investigate," he thought.

Then he remembered the lost dragon scale. There really wasn't much he could do about it as he could hardly ask anyone if they'd seen it – they would have mocked him for the rest of the trip. They weren't to know of his adventures with the dragons in Scotland during the summer holidays where he had met his best friend, Spit the dragon when they rescued Seraphina's Pearl, the dragons' name for a dragon egg, which had led to him now being counted as dragon kin. The dragons called him Petersmith.

As he looked up he saw Biffy staring oddly at something in his hand, glancing over at Peter with a very strange look on his face. As soon as he saw Peter watching him he turned away quickly and walked off.

"That was weird!" Peter muttered to himself. "Could he have…? Ridiculous! Of course not!" He answered his unfinished question. But as he pondered further over this he realised that Biffy had been one of the few people who'd been let off the rafting trip.

Biffy and his cronies used to torment him and call him the Crip because his left hand only had a thumb and two fingers on it. Spit had put an end to their bullying by magically blasting them when Peter was holding on to his dragon scale and the boys had all fallen down looking dazed and smelling rather singed. Biffy's only name for him now was "Dragon boy" and that was because one silly day he'd been day dreaming in class and answered the teacher's question by saying something about dragons. He had never heard the end of that one!

CHAPTER TWO

It was so nice to have some time to himself after lunch. He was quite comfortable about being on his own so he set off to search for where the rainbow had ended. He glanced behind him to make sure no-one was following because just recently he'd felt as if he was being watched. It was a strange feeling and he assumed his newly found dragon senses had something to do with his awareness of it.

Listening out carefully as he walked he thought he heard the scuffle of a footstep behind him, so trying to look very casual he edged towards some rocks on his left and ducked down out of sight. He stayed there for a while and just listened. There was no movement that he could hear but he decided to crouch down and move over behind some other rocks. He did this a few times until he was absolutely positive no-one was following him and then set off in the direction he had originally intended, thinking to himself that it wasn't as if he was going anywhere exciting or secretive, it was just that he wanted peace.

He finally reached the spot he had earmarked as the

end of the rainbow, puffing a little as he did because it had been an uphill walk.

There were some huge rocks to one side and he walked the whole length of them until they petered out. One end of the rocks was in the shape of a big head as if it was resting on the edge of a narrow burn which eventually dropped down to a loch filled to the brim with dirty brown water. He guessed the peat underneath it made it that way because the water in the burn was beautifully clear. The burn and loch must be fed by a loch higher up in the mountain behind him.

"These are a bit like McDragon's rocks!" announced Peter in a loud voice which echoed around him. Something bright pink was peeping out of the greyness near the cliff top and he wandered over to have a closer look.

"Wow! A frillio!" and with that he plunged his hand into the gentle fronds which were waving about in the breeze and felt that same wonderful feeling that he had done when he had last touched a frillio, of softness and comfort. His hand was pink when he pulled it out. Last time he had seen a frillio had been in the enchanted dome where he had met Spit.

"Watchya, Dragon boy! What are you doing up here!" Peter blew out a big sigh. Now he knew who'd been shadowing him. Someone he really didn't like at all.

"Oh Biffy, you made me jump. For that matter what are you doing up here? I came for some peace and quiet." Since Spit's little surprise for Biffy and his other thugs, Peter was not scared of him anymore and Biffy had been keeping his distance which must mean that he was totally flummoxed by the blast that had knocked them all down.

6

"Just keeping an eye on you, old boy! That's all."

"Well, I don't need keeping an eye on thank you. I just want some space to be on my own occasionally!"

"Shame, because I had something to show you. Never mind, I'll mosey on back to the camp." As he turned to go he suddenly twisted back again, "But what's that pink thing you were looking at?"

Peter was astounded because the frillio was something magical and Biffy shouldn't have been able to see it at all.

"Wh..what do you mean? What pink thing?!

"That pink thing that you were just touching."

"Oh… I've heard it's called a frillio." Out of the blue Peter just couldn't think of anything else to say about it.

"Really. Let me touch it too." Biffy said as he walked slowly towards the frillio.

He tentatively put his hand out to touch it, then put his fingers further into it.

"Doesn't seem to do anything at all," he announced and sauntered off in the direction of the camp.

Peter sat down with a thump.

"How can that be? He touched it but his hand didn't turn pink! But he could see it and it's magical!"

Then he realised he really did want to speak to Biffy and he jumped up to race after the other boy, calling his name as he did. He really should ask if he'd found the dragon scale although he wouldn't call it that, of course.

Biffy totally ignored him and just carried on walking steadily back down towards the camp and in the end Peter stopped chasing after him and walked disconsolately back to where the rainbow had ended.

When he got to the small clearing he sat down to rest

his back on a big rock. He could smell the peaty water of the loch nearby.

"Petersmith! I am very glad you have come back to see me," boomed a voice in his ear. He looked around him but there was no-one to see.

"I moved the end of the rainbow and hoped you would notice it and be interested enough to come here."

"Where…where are you?"

He felt the large rock behind him shift and he quickly moved away from it. The grey rocks gradually took on a humungous shape. Huge feet with long talons emerged at the end of strong big legs and then a very long tail which flicked down onto the ground raising dust around them both.

"Another dragon!!"

A big head, the length of Peter's leg, was lowered down so that Peter could see the reflection of his face in amethyst eyes. The dragon blinked. Peter blinked too, astounded as the sound of humming reverberated around them. It was a dragon's greeting. Peter joined in with it. He enjoyed dragon song.

"I am Effel. I am a dragon seer and you are Petersmith, dragon kin and friend of McDragon, Seraphina, Haribald d'Ness and Spit."

"Don't forget Popple!"

"Just so – Popple as well."

Effel looked as if she was a very ancient dragon. She was quite battered and battle scarred and her eyes had a slightly watery, filmy look to them.

Peter nodded. He was feeling rather overwhelmed.

He broke the small silence, "So do you make the pictures in the dragon seers' cave on the Isle of Harris?"

"I contribute to them, yes. There is more than one dragon seer."

"Oh. In that case do you know what has happened to McDragon please? I am very worried about him!" and he rushed into his tale of how he had misplaced or someone had stolen Spit's scale and how he needed to get in touch with Spit to see what was happening.

Effel looked at him solemnly. "Petersmith, I am unable to see specific happenings when I want to, pictures come to me in my head from time to time and I am only then able to relay them to the dragon seers' cave. What I can tell you is that I believe something has happened to your friend McDragon… something that involves wizardry and I believe that as dragon kin you will have to help him… but not yet. Firstly, we need to know far more before you can go rushing to the rescue."

"But what can I do if I cannot contact Spit? I'm unable to speak to Seraphina either as I have left her scale hidden in my room at home so it would be safe."

"Petersmith, listen to me carefully. I have had a vision where I felt great danger. You would imperil both Spit and Seraphina if you were to contact them at all through their scales because I believe you will be using what I would describe as "loose" magic. Do you understand? It is very important that you do, particularly until we can make some sense of McDragon's disappearence."

"Oh! Yes, I understand completely, Effel."

"So you can see that for the time being it does not really matter that you have had Spit's scale stolen."

CHAPTER THREE

Peter stretched out on his camp bed – his feet hung off the end. He was tired because after getting back from the end of the rainbow he'd had to join the other boys for more rafting. This time Biffy had been part of the team. It was hard work building a raft and then sculling across the loch trying to steer away from the big rocks whose slimy tips were showing above the water line. It had been wet and very cold as well. For all that, it had been fun too, particularly when one of the least liked boys had fallen into the water.

His plan today was to go back and visit Effel and her frillio when he had his break – even if it was raining. With any luck, he could nip away while Biffy was busy with his assigned chores. He wanted to know more about Effel. She was so old, old as the hills she'd said, and she must know so very much about other dragons. Surely between them they could think of a way of finding out what had happened to McDragon. Just thinking about seeing the old dragoness made him feel less alone without Spit to talk to.

After breakfast, all the boys on the trip had various projects which they had to log down in their books for school. Normally Peter would have found this quite interesting but he was keen to get away, so as soon as he was able to, he left the camp passing through the kitchen area as he did.

One of the teachers called out to him, "Peter can you collect a few sticks for kindling please?"

"Yes, sir!"

Biffy watched him leave, unable to do anything because he was peeling potatoes for lunch.

It took much less time today to reach where Effel was simply because he didn't have to dodge about trying to avoid his follower, and as he passed the frillio he touched the fronds and felt the soft magic that they contained.

"Petersmith I see you like my frillio."

"Oh, most definitely! It feels so soothing."

"Just keep an eye out because if it looks like it has flowers beginning to appear then it will not be soothing at all. If you see stalks beginning to emerge with small buds on them beware. Although it looks much like a flower, in reality it is nothing like one. The flower stalks are as sharp as a knife and can cut your hand to ribbons."

"That sounds horrid. I'll definitely watch out for that!"

The rocks seemed to melt away and finally Effel was standing there in their place. Once again Peter noticed how scarred and battered she looked.

She gave a dragon smile as she saw him watching her.

"I'm proud of these scars. They show I used to be a brave warrior dragon in my youth."

"They suit you," he answered politely. Then, "I don't mean to be rude but are you as old as the first dragons that the magicians created?"

"Not quite, but I am one of the oldest dragons still alive." And she started humming. Peter hummed along, luckily dragon song did not seem to follow any particular tune.

As their joint song began to finish there was a loud squawking from above them and then a very, windblown dishevelled crow crashed down to the ground beside Peter.

"Archie! What are you doing here?!"

Archie just lay there panting, so exhausted he was unable even to lift his head off the ground.

"Effel, this is Archie, he is Spit's friend."

"Yes, I know. Let him rest for a while and then I will try and talk to him. Petersmith, if you cross over to those rocks over there you will find a small pool of rainwater. See if you can cup some in your hands and bring it back for the poor young chappie!"

Peter scuttled off and by holding both his hands together very tightly he managed to return with a very small amount of water for the crow, who feebly lifted his head up high enough to put his beak in it. Peter ran back to fetch some more. After that was all gone he felt around in his pocket knowing he had a bit of old cake hidden away there in case he got hungry at any time. The black crow with the orange beak seemed very pleased and soon gobbled that up.

Once he had time to rest, Effel touched her snout to Archie's head just above his beady black eyes and closed her eyes. Effel's nose was as wide as the whole length of Archie's body. Peter held his breath and waited... and waited. Finally, after what seemed like hours but was probably only minutes she turned to look at him.

"What's happened?"

"It seems that Popple is unwell and neither Seraphina nor Haribald know what to do. They have tried using the frillio that Spit took to the island but that is not strong enough on its own to help. We dragons often use frillios to help cure some of our maladies and usually one frillio is sufficient. Hmmm…" Effel pondered on the situation for a while. "Petersmith, I have not flown for an age and am rather rusty but I need to go to the island and take my frillio with me to see if two will double their healing magic. Will you come along so that I can use your memories to guide me to the island? It will be in dragon time so nobody here will notice your absence. What's more you will be able to catch up with your friend Spit and we can hear all of their worries about McDragon first hand."

Without any hesitation, Peter responded with a big "Yes!"

"We will go immediately. Can you manage to carry my frillio as well as Archie? I suspect he will not have the strength for such a journey again for a few days, in fact it is quite a wonder that he managed to get here in the first place." Peter nodded his agreement as Effel continued, "First though, we must go up the track behind us as high as we can and it would save some of my energy if you could walk please."

"Ok."

The odd procession trudged slowly up the slope. Peter thought it was lucky that dragons had magic that hid them from human gaze because this huge old dragon would show up quite clearly on the horizon if anyone looked in their direction. Archie was tucked inside his jacket already sound asleep. He was quite a large crow, although surprisingly light but he took up a lot of space. The frillio resting against Peter's chest gave out waves of lovely softness which echoed throughout his body.

Once they reached the summit Peter realised he had been quite right and there was a small loch whose overflow of water trickled down feeding the burn which ran away beneath them.

It took quite a bit of scrambling and slipping before Peter finally managed to get on top of the old dragoness. He had asked her to warm him before they flew as he'd remembered just how very cold he'd got when he was with McDragon. Once she had done just that and he was on board, much the same as McDragon did, she clamped down scales onto his knees to hold him in position.

The enormous holey wings pumped slowly up and down gradually speeding up, although rather erratically and as they did it crossed his mind that he might need the relaxed feeling from the frillio if the flight was going to be a bumpy one.

"Sorry!" she called to him, "I'm not used to this."

To take off she plodded to the edge of the cliff above the lower loch and then basically threw herself off. They immediately plunged down as she tried to get her wings to work in unison. Peter felt quite scared as he imagined them crashing onto the rocks at the bottom. Eventually she had managed one or two decent flaps of her wings which stopped the fall and righted her and they turned and flew low over the loch for a while. A couple of times her feet skimmed the top of the water, which was a bit scary, but with much physical effort and panting Effel gradually started to rise higher. She struggled to maintain an even keel and at one point they passed by some seabirds that were lifting up from the loch and nearly collided with them. The gulls had squawked loudly in a blind panic and it made Peter realise that her eyesight might need some improvement. He giggled to himself at the thought that maybe she should have dragon glasses. Wow, that would be quite a strange sight.

He hoped they weren't going to come across any of the nasty squawkins which he and McDragon had encountered on a couple of their flights together. He didn't think Effel would have the strength to keep in the air and fight the squawkins off. A squawkin was something that had evolved from the gargoyles when there had been a magical wizard fight thousands of years ago. She was correct though, a little rusty was not quite the expression he would have used to describe her flying skills.

"Ermm… how many years has it been since you last flew Effel?"

"Oh, more than I can remember. As a dragon seer I do not have to move far from my rocks very often. I can catch fish which live in the small loch whenever I need to. They grow to quite a size because no-one really does much fishing there. They're very tasty!"

It was a long journey and Peter was relieved that it was in dragon time which basically meant that it slowed time down for humans so he would not be missed back at the camp at all.

Excitement bubbled in his tummy, at least he hoped it was excitement and not something gurgling about because of the bumpy ride. He was going to see Spit, who he hadn't seen in the flesh for some time and that thought was quite exciting. He'd thought he was going to have to wait until his dad next had to go to the Isle of Harris for his work. It was fun to be flying through the air with a dragon again. No-one would believe him if he told them about it.

CHAPTER FOUR

Peter couldn't help napping, despite the occasional feeling of flight sickness. He knew he should be on the lookout for squawkins, the magical but evil gargoyle-like creatures which could attack them, but the frillio was lulling him into a feeling of security.

"Petersmith, please can you picture the island in your head now!" Effel called to him and he came to and realised they were flying over the dark sea.

He immediately imagined what Seraphina's island looked like and it must have helped Effel because she did a steep turn to the right, banking as she did. Peter leaned slightly into the turn looking around them. There was nothing to be seen on the horizon apart from a few birds. He could feel Archie's chest lifting up and down gently as the crow still snoozed contentedly inside his jacket.

"How many dragon seers are there Effel?"

"Not too many I believe. We are in very small groups which look after various dragon seer caves. My pod is linked to the one you have seen on the Isle of Harris."

"I take it that you didn't have a vision that something was going to happen to McDragon?"

"No, we each seemed to have a vision of something unbalancing the magic of the dragons and a feeling of danger but nothing specific relating to McDragon." He felt her wobble about a little and then she said, "Petersmith, I think that is your island over there on the horizon!"

He felt sure she must be right but there was no way he could see that far ahead of them. Maybe she was long sighted. As they closed the gap between them and what Peter could now see was an island, she turned sharply angling downwards. As they neared the familiar rocks he spotted the place where McDragon had landed with him each time they had visited.

Time to hang on, he thought, gritting his teeth and gripping grimly to one of the battered scales, all of which were upright or trying to be upright, down her long neck. They were quite floppy, not like those of McDragon which were all firm to touch.

It turned out to be a very, very, rough landing and she actually splatted down flat on her chin and skidded along on her belly for a few yards in the dust landing in a heap near some rocks.

"Well done Effel! Considering you haven't done that for such a long time that wasn't as bad as it could have been!"

"Thank you, laddie! You are most kind!"

As she released her scales his knees were freed and he lifted one of his legs over her back to begin to slip carefully down to the ground, at the same time making sure he did not squash Archie. Then he heard the thumping of dragon feet and before he knew it a small dragon had knocked him to the ground.

"Petersmith!! How do you do?!!!" which was their special greeting to one another.

"Very well thank you Spit! And how do you do?"

"Very well thank you Petersmith!" and they both started to giggle. Peter let a flustered Archie out of his coat very quickly as well as pushing the frillio to safety before Spit pounced on him and rolled him about in the dust. Effel just stared at them in amazement, her head remaining flat on the ground.

Once things had finally quietened down Peter asked where Popple was.

"I will take you to her, Seraphina and Haribald d'Ness are with her. They are very worried about her indeed." And Spit thundered away from him.

Peter snatched up the frillio and traipsed after his dragon friend with Effel hobbling behind him. Archie flew above them.

When they approached some rocks with an overhang Peter could see the shape of Seraphina in the shade. Haribald was next to her.

"Petersmith, it is good to see you, and Effel, it has been a long time!" The four dragons all looked at one another and then the dragon song began quietly at first and finished in a humming crescendo. Peter joined in and even Archie squawked along.

"We have brought my frillio in the hope that its magic can join with the frillio you have to see if that will help mend your little one."

Poor Popple did not look well at all. Her head was

hanging down low and she obviously felt so ill that she could only nod bravely at Peter to acknowledge him.

Peter placed his hand gently on her head and gave it a little stroke. It upset him greatly to see her like this. Last time he had been with her had been a few days after she had hatched from the dragon Pearl which he and Spit and Archie had rescued from the evil magician, McMuran. She'd been tiny then. Peter had been given the honour of being the one to name her and he decided on Popsicle, or Popple for short, which suited her as she was always popping about.

"Petersmith, please can you put one of the frillios near to Popple's head?" Seraphina asked quietly. When he had done that she told Popple to rest her head on that frillio and then pushed the second one up against her nose so she could breathe in through it.

They all waited impatiently to see if anything happened. For a while there was no movement at all and then Popple's face began to infuse with pink and the colour gradually spread down her whole little body finally reaching her tail and going right along each small leg to the very ends of her talons. The tension went out of the tiny dragon as she relaxed and she appeared to sleep.

"That is a good sign," announced Effel. "A very good sign indeed!" The other two adult dragons nodded their enormous heads in agreement, looking quite relieved.

Seraphina told Spit and Peter to go away and try and use up some of Spit's energy for a while as they watched over Popple. After that they would have a dragon pow wow.

Spit raced away as soon as he was told to go and Peter soon realised why Seraphina said he had energy to burn as Spit turned to run at him and knock him down. They tumbled around like two small boys. Peter was quite grubby and dusty when eventually they rested near one another. He was quite worn out but he rather thought that was not the case for Spit.

"I have lost your scale Spit – I think Biffy might have stolen it."

"That would explain why I have been getting a fuzzy feeling in my chest and imagine a boy is peering at me. Now I know I can ignore it. Can you get it back again? I think the gap on my chest will be too big if you take another scale?"

They both looked at Spit's chest where Peter had had to take a second scale after he had lost the first one he'd been given during the fight with some squawkins who had attacked McDragon and Peter previously. Spit was right, three scales would leave a very big unprotected area on his chest.

"I'll do my best but even if I do, Effel says that we shouldn't use the scales at the moment to contact one another because they use loose magic and she has had a vision that shows this is dangerous."

"Oh… OK. But I miss speaking to you Petersmith!"

"I miss our conversations as well Spit. I get quite lonely, but at least you have Popple and the other dragons with you."

"That's true, but I am often in trouble for not concentrating on improving my dragon skills," Spit answered forlornly.

"If I can get it back we can use it as soon as Effel says it is safe to do so. Shall we go to see if the others are ready to have this pow wow?"

Spit sniggered he liked the idea of a pow wow.

CHAPTER FIVE

It was a great relief to see that Popple was awake and eating a shiny small fish when they reached the area where the overhanging rocks were. That meant she was on the road to recovery. As they joined the other dragons they could hear Effel, "It's quite worrying that it took two frillios to help Popple mend. I am worried that some wizard is messing with us. Someone, somewhere must be jinxing the magic."

Haribald nodded sagely in agreement. "It does all feel wrong. It is also very odd that McDragon has not come here. I flew over his rocks on Harris earlier this morning but something seemed out of place when I did. I couldn't see him but then there was something tickling my magic at the same time. I came away immediately I felt danger."

"Perhaps a visit to the dragon seers' cave should be made," suggested Seraphina. "What do you think Effel? It may be that one of your partner seers has had a vision and recorded it there."

"It's worth a try but I know I will not be able to fly there soon as it will take all my strength to return this young laddie to his camp. I need to practice my flying a little bit more in the hope that it will get easier." As she spoke Effel's eyes seemed to glaze over and she went into a trance. There was silence as they all waited… and waited.

"What is happening?" whispered Peter. He was rather worried that Effel was taking a turn for the worse and she wouldn't be able to take him back to the camp.

"Just wait," Haribald instructed him quietly.

Time almost seemed to stand still until she finally opened her big amethyst eyes and called urgently, "Get under cover, I sense something bad is coming this way!"

There was a big dragon scramble as they all squashed themselves against the rocks where the overhang was.

"I felt something … I do not know what is coming but we should be prepared!"

Even as she spoke there was a rush of wings overhead and then three red squawkins flew into view in formation, one at the front and two on either side just a little way back. Fortunately, they came from behind the overhang so from that angle could not see any of the dragons nor the small boy who was squashed at the back next to Popple.

As the squawkins crossed above the small island they gave out their terrible shrieks which had Peter pressing his hands to his ears. The lead squawkin left the formation and swept down to drop something onto the ground and it returned to the head of the squawkins and they all left as suddenly as they had arrived, their high pitched calls slicing through the airwaves. It was rather like someone scraping their nails down a blackboard. Horrible! The sound gradually faded away as they passed back the way they had come.

23

The dragons stayed where they were in case it was a trap until finally Haribald snuck his head out and looked over at the direction the squawkins were heading.

"OK… they have definitely gone, thank goodness. Let me go and investigate what has been left for us. It seems your hideaway is no secret any longer, Seraphina!"

Peter watched quietly as the big dragon circled the package, sniffing and peering down at the squawkins' "present". He did not look happy when he called for the others to come out.

"Do not touch it! Let me know what you think of this and we'll see if we all agree."

Peter had no idea at all, it didn't smell too good and there was something like a translucent elastic band strapped over the green pile.

He looked over at Spit and muttered, "It smells like poo – a very big poo at that!"

"Ah, so you agree with the rest of us Petersmith!" said Effel.

"Do I… don't you like the smell either?"

"Petersmith this "poo", as you call it, has a distinct aroma of a particular dragon, McDragon. We all know what McDragon smells like."

"Well, I never really took any notice of anything like that!"

"There is a definite reminder of McDragon in that little package. The wrapping holding it together, however, is another matter. There is a waft of magic there and it is not good magic!"

"Why has this been dropped here then, Effel?"

"I feel it is a message for us. Is that how you see it Seraphina?"

24

Seraphina nodded her big beautiful head slowly, "Yes, indeed Seer Effel. Whoever sent it knew that we were here and is trying to pull us into looking for McDragon. I fear that they may have him captured somewhere which is why he has not been visiting us."

"It will be a trap!" Haribald joined in, "Although not a very well baited trap I admit, but a trap for all that."

"How come whoever it is wants you to leave the island?"

"A magician cannot send magic to us here because we are totally surrounded by water. We will have to remain close to the island or risk getting caught ourselves."

"I've a question please?" They all looked enquiringly at Petersmith, "They might not be able to land here but the squawkins could swoop down and grab Popple couldn't they?"

The three adult dragons looked at one another nodding their heads in agreement looking horrified.

"We will have to make sure that Popple is never left unattended!" announced Seraphina, "I couldn't bear it if she was taken from me after waiting for such a long time for her Pearl to be found!"

"Also," Peter added, "if you cannot leave the island because of the trap how will you find McDragon?" They turned in unison and peered down at Peter.

"Wh…what is it?"

"Petersmith, it seems that you may yet again have to prove your worth as dragon kin and be the one to find McDragon and rescue him!"

CHAPTER SIX

Peter was soon back at the camp, deep in thought. Again, it seemed it would be his task to aid the dragons or else they would have to risk their lives trying to evade the trap which had been set for them. The concensus of opinion was that it was likely that an able magician had imprisoned McDragon and it could well be McMuran who'd done that. He must have avoided the fire that had been burning when Peter had last seen him.

"Hey, Dragon boy! Where have you been? You've been gone for a very long time!"

Peter looked surprised… how come Biffy had noticed his absence? They'd been using dragon time. He'd made sure he had collected a big pile of sticks for kindling on the way back from Effel's rocks to the camp and the teacher had said he appreciated Peter's speed in returning with it.

"Did you miss me then Biffy?" He stared Biffy out and the bully boy was the first to drop his eyes and mumble, "No matter Dragon boy, I just noticed you hadn't brought the sticks back pronto."

Peter shrugged his shoulders, "Well teacher thought I was quite quick."

Biffy looked rather surprised but said nothing further.

* * *

There were only just a few days left before they were due to return home from the camp. Peter felt he'd been there ages, but in fact it was only about five days so far. Before he had met Effel, Peter had been longing to go home but now he wanted to be somewhere close to Effel who could take him to the other dragons in the hope that they could come up with a plan for him to look for McDragon. Biffy seemed to be dogging his footsteps and it was very hard to try and escape his watchful eyes.

At every break time Peter would try a different route up to where Effel was. Sometimes she just spoke to him without changing into a dragon and sometimes she was there waiting for him in her great old dragon body. He always had the sense that she was very, very, old and incredibly knowledgeable, which naturally she was considering how long she'd lived.

Today he snuck out of the tent and went past the kitchen area, then dodged around the back of that tent to try and trick Biffy into thinking he had gone the other way. Every so often he would stand still and just wait and then set off in a very circuitous route. It all took extra time when he would rather be talking to Effel so he was relieved when at last he jogged puffing into the small clearing where she was waiting for him, standing looking out over the loch below her.

"Petersmith… I 've been waiting for you."

"Sorry Effel but I had to try and lay a false trail for Biffy because he keeps following me."

"I've been thinking about that boy. I find it hard to sense where he is much of the time. I can feel you though quite clearly."

"I wonder if he has Spit's scale and it tickles him somehow making him want to know more about it."

"Quite possibly. I was thinking about that. In an emergency, I think you might be able to use him to contact Spit via the scale. I have this strange feeling that as I cannot sense where Biffy is, the wizard might not be able to intercept any messages from him either."

"But that would mean explaining to him what the scale is and knowing Biffy he would just laugh and laugh."

"He may surprise you yet. Has he ever been interested in you this much before?"

"No, not really, only when he was bullying me but Spit put an end to that!"

"Hmm… just keep an eye on him, you never know if he may be of help to you."

"OK, if I have to I will. I'd do anything to help you dragons!"

He stayed and chatted to her for as long as he could and then after having a little touch of the frillio dashed off down to the camp following the same route he'd taken to get there.

Biffy was by the cook tent as he got there.

"Hey Dragon boy, where have you been?"

"I just went for a walk Biffy, why the interest?"

Biffy just grunted and walked off. He always seemed to be on his own these days, which was another mystery.

CHAPTER SEVEN

It was their last day at the camp and they were all tidying up. Fortunately, they didn't have to take the tents down but just leave everything ready for the next school who were arriving the following day. Peter had nearly finished packing his rucksack and had strapped his sleeping bag on to it when he looked out of the tent flap. There had been some more fine rain and he spotted another rainbow. As he watched it the end moved, as it had before, and yet again finished up at Effel's special place. He took it as a sign that she was summoning him so after first checking that Biffy was fully occupied with his packing, Peter slipped out of the tent and set off at full speed straight up to where the end of the rainbow had been. He noticed as he ran how much faster he'd become. It was unlikely that Biffy, if he started out behind him, would be fast enough to catch him.

Effel was there waiting patiently.

"Oh good, I hoped you would realise I wanted to see you. Hop on laddie and let's go for a last ride together! Wait while I warm you first, it's easier to do it here before we go up any higher."

Once that was done they clambered up the track to the higher loch and then he was soon on her back with her side scales locked firmly down on his knees. She plodded to the edge of the cliff just as she had before and again more or less threw herself off of it. They dropped downwards, faster and faster before she managed to somehow get control of her holey wings and they flattened out skimming over the loch. The water did look beautiful but Peter most definitely had no desire to feel the coldness of it if they fell in. He looked back towards the cliff top they had just left and he could have sworn he could see a boy standing there. They had left just in time!

"Where are we going Effel?"

"I thought you'd like to visit your friend for a brief time and then we can also find out how Popple is doing, although I had a vision which shows me that she is much recovered."

"Oh, thank you Effel! That's amazing! I do miss speaking to Spit!"

Peter couldn't see Effel's face but had he been able to he would have noticed how much pleasure his thanks gave her. He could feel the unevenness of her wings going up and down and he just hoped it was going to be an uneventful journey.

After the long flight their landing was just as bad as before, but Peter didn't say a word, he was just happy to have arrived in one piece. So was his stomach, which had not enjoyed the choppy ride at all.

Once she had landed in a huge messy heap, panting heavily and trying to catch her breath, Peter hopped off to be bowled down immediately by a very excited young dragon who rolled him over and over. When they finally came to a halt against a rock, Spit picked himself up and solemnly said, "How do you do Petersmith?"

Peter responded, "Very well thank you Spit, and how do you do?" he bowed and Spit bowed back.

"Very well thank you Petersmith. I am very happy to see you again."

"Me too!" Archie swooped down from up high and gave Peter a little peck on the nose. He'd opted to remain on the island with Spit so that he could be sent as a runner, or in his case, flyer, with any message for Effel.

As they finished their hellos there was a scuffling sound from the right and Popple came scuttling over to see Peter and prodded him with her snout. He smiled with delight to see that she looked quite well and gave her a big hug and a kiss on the top of her scaly head. He had to bend down very low as her head didn't quite come up to his knees.

Behind him he could hear Effel dragging herself up onto her feet and then they followed her towards the overhang where Seraphina and Haribald were waiting for them. Seraphina began to hum the dragon greeting and Haribald joined in as did Spit and Popple, much to Peter's surprise. Her hum was quite high pitched but still in tune with the other dragons. It amused Peter that Effel's hum was a little off key but then when Peter joined in with them, as he liked to do, he wasn't that sure that he was properly in tune with them either.

Group hum over Popple nudged Peter again and he bent down and gave her muzzle a stroke – she almost purred like a cat when he did and then rolled over to show her tummy which was a lighter colour than the rest of her and although it was covered in tiny scales it was still soft to touch.

Spit giggled, "She likes you doing that! I think I'm a bit too big for a tummy rub though. Do you think I have grown Petersmith?"

"Definitely Spit. It won't be long before you're as big as McDragon."

Spit puffed himself up looking very proud and started to strut about. Even Popple laughed when she saw him. He reminded Peter of a peacock showing off his beautiful feathers.

Effel interrupted all this frivolity by asking if they had received any other offerings from the squawkins.

"No, nothing more. My guess is that the magician would hope that it is enough to make us rush to try and get McDragon back. He must be fairly certain that we can't succeed or why else would they bait the trap like that? I would think he is totally unaware of Petersmith being here." Seraphina answered.

Effel humrumphhed and then told them she'd had another vision only last night and it appeared to reconfirm that Petersmith might again be the one to mount McDragon's rescue.

"But, Effel, I don't know when I'll next be in Scotland. My dad hasn't said anything about it." He thought for a while. "I will ask him when I get home tomorrow. But how will I let you know?"

"You may need to use your bully boy Biffy to do that."
"What!!!"

"Spit cannot give you another scale because that will

leave his heart area unprotected until his other scales grow over the gap. At worst, you could contact Seraphina through her scale, but as I told you before, that is loose magic and the message could be intercepted by the magician and he could possibly use it as a link to her. However," Effel continued in her gruff voice, "perhaps you could somehow trick Biffy so that he passes the message on. You seem to feel sure that he is the one that has the scale."

"Yes, I am pretty certain he does because I cannot see why else he would want to keep shadowing me and he's often looking down at something in is hand. What's more Spit said he felt something coming from the scale."

"Well, if you can try and contact us that way it would be best because I do not believe any wizard would be able to understand a message that was not meant for them if it came from someone as non-magical as Biffy."

"I definitely won't use it. You never know you may get a vision to let you know I'm in Scotland."

"If only my foresight worked like that!"

He spent the rest of his precious time on the island with Spit. Popple trailed them everywhere and sometimes joined in with the bundle they might be having if they were not being too rough. Peter taught both dragons how to play tag. He thought it might be a good way to halt being rolled in the dirt all the time. Popple loved it. She was very quick on her tiny feet and Spit also enjoyed being able to charge around the small clearing and hiding behind the rocks. It was a very funny sight indeed because Spit always forgot that his tail would be sticking out from where he was hiding or his scaly back would be showing above the rocks he crouched behind. Peter didn't tell him this because it was good to have some secrets that might help him win occasionally. The only trouble was that once Spit was found he would pounce on Peter in his excitement.

It was sad when he had to leave and he gave each, and every one of them a big hug and an especially big kiss to Popple. Even Haribald didn't seem to mind him doing this. He had no idea when he would get to see them again.

CHAPTER EIGHT

It was good to find his dad waiting for him when the coach finally dropped the children off at the school gate but he noticed that there was no-one there for Biffy who shouldered his rucksack and started to trudge home. Peter's dad stopped by the boy and offered him a lift and Biffy looked very relieved to accept, he was obviously tired, much like Peter was. Not that he said anything on the way apart from giving directions to where he lived. He clambered out and politely said thank you, just glancing Peter's way the one time as he left them.

"He seems a nice boy," his dad said, "and quiet with it. Is he one of your friends?"

"Not really dad, I didn't even know he lived where he does until we gave him the lift."

They chatted about the school trip and Scotland and as they pulled into the drive his dad turned to him and said, "Well Peter, you said you fancied going to Harris again."

"Oh yes, I'd love to dad. When?"

"As soon as you break up for half term. It'll be just you and me this time as it's a long way for your mum and

Alice to go just for a week and they can have fun at home together. I know that it's very soon to travel again after you've just got back from your trip so I quite understand if you feel you should say no."

"Oh, I would definitely like to come please!"

"That's settled then."

He felt the excitement rising in him and, also the worry that now he would have to think how to tackle Biffy about the scale. He just hoped his dragon senses would help him with a plan because, for the moment, he couldn't see any way at all that would lead to him bringing the subject up without being direct about it.

For all that he ran straight into the house and gave his mum a big kiss and cuddle and felt happy enough to ruffle Alice's hair as she sat at the dining room table doing her homework.

It was good to be home and even better now he knew he was returning to Scotland so soon.

* * *

He set off to school nice and early the next day, content in the knowledge that he wouldn't be bullied by Biffy and his band of thugs as before. The only niggle was the worry that there were only a few days left before the end of term and he had no idea how he was going to get a message to Spit.

Concentrating on lessons throughout the following days was difficult because his mind kept imagining different scenarios with Biffy. It seemed that the project that they had to complete over half term was writing about what they had got out of the trip to Scotland and what new skills they'd learned while they were there. Peter smiled to himself because he could hardly write about flying with Effel and battling with travel sickness!

The final bell on the last school day eventually rang and he still had absolutely no idea in his head of a plan when he plodded along to his locker to gather anything he needed to take with him. As he reached the locker area he could see Biffy ahead of him chatting to some other boys with his bag wide open next to where Peter had to stand to reach into his space. The maps of the area of Scotland where they had visited were resting on top of the bag. What if? Without any more thought he grabbed the two top maps which both had Biffy's name on them and he stuffed them quickly into his own bag and sauntered off towards the doors and out onto the playground. There was no hue and cry following him – no-one had noticed a thing. As he walked home he formulated a plan.

The next morning after breakfast he told his mum he was going for a walk to have a think about his project. He would do his packing when he got back as they were leaving that afternoon when his dad got back and driving throughout the night as they had done before. His dad was going to have to do all the driving himself this time, although he did tell Peter he would probably have to stop now and then to have a short nap.

It was lucky they'd taken Biffy home the other day because before that he'd had no idea of where he lived. He strolled along Biffy's street looking for his house. As he arrived he could see the side gate was open so he walked quietly through it intending to knock at the back door. As he almost reached the door it was flung wide open and there was a very angry man standing with his back to Peter, his arm held by Biffy who was shouting, "Leave her alone, don't hit her dad, please don't hit her anymore!!"

Peter stood stock still very shocked and he stepped back a bit so he couldn't be seen but at the same time could still see through to where Biffy was.

"Don't you talk to me like that boy!" and Peter was very upset to see the big man close his fist and pull it back and whack Biffy again and again on his arm, chest and then his head.

Biffy didn't utter a sound, he just took the beating.

Peter had a quick think and shuffled back as fast as he could through the gate up to the front door and rang the doorbell very firmly. He did it again just to make sure it was heard.

"Get that woman!" the order was so loud that Peter could hear it very clearly through the closed front door. A very timid looking dishevelled woman opened the door. Peter could see that just the effort of opening the door was hurting her.

Peter spoke very loudly, "Is Biffy there please? I have something for him from the school."

From the noise coming from further into the house he guessed that Biffy's dad had let go of him. Then the door opened further and Biffy stepped out onto the front door step. He looked a bit battered.

"Oh, there you are Biffy. Are you OK? What happened to you?" knowing full well what had actually taken place.

"I just fell down the stairs, that's all. I'm fine."

"OK, can you just come out here please? I have

something of yours I believe," Peter said stepping back down the path. Biffy followed, glancing behind him as he did. The front door closed with a slam and Peter guessed the man, who he supposed was Biffy's dad must have kicked the door shut.

Biffy followed him to the gate. "What do you want Dragon boy?"

Peter pulled the maps he had taken from the bag out of the inside of his jacket. "I found these and they have your name on them. I would think you need them for your half term project so as I'm off to Scotland with my dad this afternoon I thought I'd better get them to you now."

"Thank you, Dragon boy. That was kind of you." He looked thoughtful.

"By the way Biffy, I lost something in the tent while we were at camp, something grey and a bit like a flat shell. You didn't happen to notice it did you? It was a souvenir from Scotland."

Biffy put his hand into his jacket pocket and seemed to be feeling something there.

"No… sorry," he mumbled.

"Oh, that's a shame, I would have liked to have taken it with me to the Isle of Harris today," Peter announced clearly, "Dad is driving up there this afternoon and taking me with him."

"Lucky you, so you get to go to Harris again. I liked being in Scotland but I've never been to the Isle of Harris." Biffy still seemed to be fingering something in his pocket and Peter just hoped that the message would now have got through to Spit. Biffy suddenly looked shocked and pulled his hand out of his pocket very suddenly.

Peter nodded. He could only guess that meant that Spit had sent a message back to him so he smiled saying, "Oh well, see you around Biffy!" and sauntered off back the way he had come towards his home. He hoped that Biffy's dad didn't decide to continue battering him when he went back inside but there wasn't much he could do about it if he did.

CHAPTER NINE

Early that afternoon Peter helped his dad put their bags in the boot of the car along with some food that mum had packed up for them. They could supplement this by popping into the shops in Tarbert.

His dad got into the driving seat and started the engine up, eager to be off, while Peter nipped back indoors for a couple of things he'd left lying on the bed. He raced up the stairs two at a time and snatched up his binoculars and camera and then leapt back down and out of the front door, making a mental check that he had everything. He knew the most important thing he needed to take was Seraphina's scale and that was safely tucked away in the bottom of his bag inside a folded up teeshirt. He'd made sure his fingers didn't accidentally touch it as he wrapped it up.

Slamming the boot shut as he passed it without bothering to look inside he jumped quickly into the passenger seat as his mum hurried out of the house holding a small carrier bag which she passed in to Peter, saying it was egg sandwiches and some cake which made

Peter laugh – they always had egg sandwiches when they went on a journey. She walked quickly round to the driver's window to say another farewell to his dad. Alice smiled at them from the doorstep, watching them reverse out into the road and when Peter looked back towards the house he could see his mum was still on the pavement waving.

It wasn't long before they hit the motorway and then started to head towards Glasgow. After that it was the long drive along many winding roads in the dusk. Peter nodded off until he felt the car slow down and he opened his eyes to see they were pulling into a garage.

"Petrol stop," said his dad. "Do you need the loo at all as it will be quite a while before we stop again, unless of course I feel tired and have to pull over for a nap?"

"Probably a good idea dad, I won't be a minute."

The tank was filled up and the petrol paid for by the time Peter returned to the car just as his dad was flipping up the boot lid intending to retrieve something from a bag. As he did he stepped back and stood open mouthed in shock.

"Who are you?" Peter heard him say.

A dark haired tousled head appeared over the boot.

"Biffy! What are you doing there?"

"Oh, it's the boy we dropped home the other day."

"Yes, he's in my class at school."

"Well, it's too far to take him back home so we had better call his parents and let them know where he is for starters. They must be worried sick!"

Biffy looked rather shamefaced and then clambered very slowly and stiffly out of the boot. He looked incredibly uncomfortable, it couldn't have been a nice journey for him crunched up with the bags the whole time they'd been travelling. He was shivering, despite wearing a coat.

"Oh, you're freezing boy! Get into the car where it's warmer! Peter pass him the rug to wrap around him and then give him a warm drink out of the thermos flask and a sandwich."

"Th...thank you!" muttered Biffy.

"Surely you realised that you would get cold in the boot? There's no heating in there at all."

"I thought my coat would be warm enough."

"Did you mean to come all the way to Harris with us?" asked Peter.

"It was a spur of the moment thing. It seemed like a good idea at the time as I just wanted to get away for a while," was the woeful reply and when Peter looked at his face he saw that he had a black eye which looked very swollen and must be painful. His eyelid would not close down on his eye properly.

"How did you get that?" asked his dad pointing at the eye.

"I fell down the stairs."

"No, you didn't Biffy, your dad hit you, I saw him. That's why I knocked on the front door. I wanted to stop him."

Biffy looked a bit tearful as he nodded, "Well I did something wrong and he was angry."

"We can talk about that later but for now what's your home telephone number so we can ring and let them know you are safe and sound. My guess is that you'll have to stay with us until we return at the end of the week."

"Thank you, sir," Biffy responded politely and he told them his phone number.

43

Peter's dad used his mobile phone to call and the conversation was very terse. His dad did offer to put Biffy on a train to come home but suggested that it might be easier all round if he stayed and kept Peter company. Biffy then had to speak to his father and explain that he would like to stay with them in Scotland. That was a very short conversation indeed.

It was all finally agreed, Biffy would stay with them in Harris.

Peter glared at Biffy, he might feel sorry for him but he needed to be free to start his search for McDragon as soon as possible. Then he realised that there was one bright side to this – if he needed to pass a message to Spit he could use Biffy somehow for that. His mum always said every cloud had a silver lining, and as usual she was correct.

Biffy ate rather a lot of the egg sandwiches as they continued with their journey and he also ate more than his fair share of the chocolate that Peter had been sent back into the garage to buy. It seemed that the last meal Biffy had had was his breakfast due to the fact that he had wanted to keep out of his dad's way until he'd calmed down.

Conversation was rather sparse, Peter could think of nothing to say and Peter's dad was concentrating on the sharp bends in the darkness and looking out for random deer in case they shot across the road suddenly.

It was a relief to finally reach Uig and dad stopped the car in the ferry line and put his head back so he could rest his eyes. It was very early in the morning.

Peter thought he would go and look and see if the seals were still around and Biffy clambered out of the car to go with him and ease his legs.

As they walked Peter asked, "What on earth possessed you to get into the boot like that? We might not have opened it until the next day and you would have been trapped."

"I just had this weird feeling that I should come along to see you. It was very strange because I have no idea at all why that should be. Not like me at all!"

Peter wondered if dragon magic had something to do with that but he didn't say that of course.

"When I saw the boot open, I just climbed in without much thought really. I was feeling a bit battered so it was nice to just lay there quietly and once the car drove off I nodded off for quite a while." Then he pointed, "Oh, look! There's a seal... and another one! I've never seen a wild seal before. Wow!"

"They're good to look at, aren't they? They sometimes come into the bay where we stay."

"I'll love seeing that. Sorry I've barged in on your trip with your dad Dragon boy."

An apology from the bully was definitely a first!

CHAPTER TEN

Peter was very happy to get back to his old room in the cottage. Biffy was going to sleep in what had been Alice's room. They had stopped in Tarbert when they disembarked from the ferry so they could get some spare clothes for Biffy – he couldn't last the week with just what he was wearing. There was an amazing shop there which seemed to stock everything except food. Biffy didn't seem to mind what the clothes were that they bought, he was just fascinated to see all the different things that were on sale.

After that they went into the grocer's shop to buy some meat for a couple of evening meals and other bits and bobs, like fresh bread and porridge. Peter had been pleased to see his dad had bought some more of the black pudding which they'd enjoyed eating at breakfast occasionally when they were last here. It had been yummy with fried eggs and tomato sauce.

There had only been two trips to and from the car to carry their luggage and supplies this time because there were only two of them with bags. That had been another surprise for Biffy, it hadn't occurred to him that they couldn't park by the house but had to walk along the cliff top instead. He was panting quite badly after the second trek back to the cottage as he just wasn't fit and he had to keep wiping his arm across his forehead to mop up the sweat which was forming there. Peter on the other hand was very happy to find that he wasn't breathing fast at all, which was quite an improvement on the last time.

His dad made them some cheese and salad baps for lunch and Peter asked if he could take his down to the rocks to eat. He was a little disappointed but unsurprised to find Biffy tagging along with him.

The tide was out so they climbed over the rocks and peered into the pools to watch small crabs scuttling about under the water. Peter really wanted to clamber over to the rocks where McDragon usually was. It used to be amazing to watch the black and gold rocks melt away to reveal a fully grown enormous dragon. McDragon was bigger than Effel and she was quite a size!

Eventually Peter managed to somehow guide Biffy over to the dragon rocks and then he put his hand on one of them, pretending to steady himself as he did. He was sad to find that they felt cold. If McDragon had been here they would have been slightly warm to the touch.

"What's this Dragon boy?" Biffy handed him a long length of something quite strange looking but flexible. As Peter touched it he got that tingle at the back of his neck which told him it had something to do with magic.

"I'm not sure Biffy."

"Well it feels strange! Does it feel odd to you?"

Peter just stared at the other boy.

"You can feel something from this?"

"Yes! What is it?"

"I really don't know but it seems familiar somehow. Maybe it's something like a stinging nettle and that's why it affects you."

He examined it more closely thinking hard as the tingle now ran up and down his spine. Yes, that was it, he'd seen it tied round that strange parcel of dragon poo that had been dropped on the island where Seraphina and Haribald were.

"We should keep this safe!" he announced and put it into his pocket. "I collect things like this," but as he zipped up the pocket he felt something tickling his memory. He knew he'd come across this somewhere else, apart from the island where Seraphina was now, but the question was where?

Time to change the subject, he thought in case Biffy asked some awkward questions. He sat down and leaned his back against McDragon's rocks opening his packet of two rolls. Biffy copied him.

"What's your real name Biffy? I can't imagine your mum and dad called you Biffy when you were a baby."

Biffy looked embarrassed and there was silence for a while. Then he met Peter's eyes sheepishly. "You won't tell anyone at school will you if I tell you?"

"No I won't. It's not anyone else's business."

"It's Cyril Blaize." He muttered quietly, "Cyril!!! And Blaize like a horse! I thought Biffy sounded much more macho!"

"I have a friend in Scotland who was called Wee Spittle by other people and he hated it. I call him Spit and he likes that." Peter smiled as he thought of Spit and why he'd been called Wee Spittle. It was because being a young dragon he'd tried to blow fire out of his nostrils and what came out instead were a few sparks and a great deal of dragon snot which splattered out in all directions.

"That's a funny name. Did his parents name him that?"

"Oh no. But that's a story for another day."

They sat companionably in silence while they munched on their baps.

It was a very strange feeling to be sitting beside Biffy without bracing himself for some bullying. Very strange indeed! They'd never had a conversation at all in the past.

"What's that bird over there, Dragon boy?"

"That's an oyster catcher. Aren't they pretty and quite noisy? There always seems to be two of them. And see that big white bird in the sky, just keep your eyes on it and watch it do a fabulous dive into the sea."

There was a big splosh as the gannet dived into the water coming up a short while later holding a small fish in its beak.

Biffy was totally absorbed in watching it and the other sea life around them.

CHAPTER ELEVEN

When Peter woke up the next day all he could hear was the gentle sound of the small waves which rippled on the sea. He automatically looked out the window to peer over at McDragon's rocks, but sadly there was still no sign of the fabulous dragon.

While he dressed, he could feel that niggling feeling that deep down was the memory of where he'd previously seen the silken rope-like stuff they had found by the rocks. It was annoying that he just couldn't remember.

He crept down the stairs and shot out of the house, grabbing his coat as he did, much as he had done every day when they had last stayed at the cottage. He was on his own at long last and it felt good.

The otter was munching on a big fish near the rocks on the other side of the small beach and he could hear the oyster catchers calling to one another. It was so peaceful and he felt quite at home.

He made his way over to McDragon's rocks so he could have a thorough exploration of the area and see if there were any clues to what had happened to McDragon.

He really missed the big dragon who'd taken him flying at this time in the morning, always using dragon time so that his family didn't notice that he was gone so long.

There was nothing to be found around the rocks, which were still very cold to the touch and feeling rather dispirited he started his walk back to the house. Then he had his light bulb moment! That was it, the silken rope looked like parts of the swannees, which had popped up and down in the magical dome that was on McMuran's island where he'd discovered Spit. Spit found it amusing to toss pine cones in the air above where they were situated. Their heads would pop up and down as they tried to catch the seeds which fell out of them. The swannees heads and necks looked rather like flamingos which couldn't move from the spot except they were more plant forms rather than bird or even animal. Were there swannees in other parts of Scotland or just on that island? He needed to ask Spit about it, but how on earth was he going to do that without letting on to Biffy what he was talking about and, even more so, to whom?

As he mooched about a sudden gust of wind knocked into him and he had to grab onto some nearby rocks to stop overbalancing and ending up in the sea. A large shadow crossed over him at the same time. Then there was a crashing of stones on the beach and what sounded like something skidding heavily before whatever it was collided very noisily with the rocks. Something bright pink spun into the air and bounced down into a pool nearby, splashing Peter with the cold seawater as it did. Peter could hear a lot of heavy panting and groaning and was astounded to see Effel in front of him as she peered around looking rather befuddled and dazed. Her big eyes seemed to be looking towards one another in a very cross-eyed fashion.

"Effel, what are you doing here?"

"I thought you might need some help Petersmith."

Effel struggled to her feet and stood there very shakily, wobbling from side to side. Peter kept well back, there was no way he wanted to be crushed by a huge old dragon.

"Wait a while and I'll just get my bearings. That was a bit of a tricky landing," she said, "and not one of my best!"

Peter, who hadn't ever seen her make a really good landing tried not to smile. "I should say. I'm just glad I wasn't with you," pronounced Peter. "At least you know you can only get better."

"Quite so Petersmith. Quite so."

"Effel, I thought you dragons believed that whoever took McDragon might have made a trap to catch another one of you?"

"I believe my seer magic will help keep me safe," she replied shaking herself making her holey wings shudder as she did, throwing lots of small stones and sand into the air. Sand and bits of rock toppled down from her big head splashing into the nearby pools. Peter had to cover his head with his hands so he didn't get covered with the debris.

Once he'd dusted himself off and settled down again, there was a nasty sulphuric smell as Effel started to heal herself with her spit. The cuts caused by sliding along the beach and rocks hissed and steamed and then sealed themselves. It was a shame that the dragon spit healing only worked on dragons in that way and not humans.

Meanwhile Peter went to the rock pool and gathered up the frillio which was lying rather forlornly in the water. Already small minnows were prodding at it to see if it was edible. His hands were soothed by the lovely balmy feeling as he carried it back to where Effel was administering to herself.

"Why have you brought the frillio with you Effel?"

"Well, I thought we should test it out on your friend, Biffy again."

"Why him?!"

"We know that Biffy can see and feel magic but how does it affect him? I need to be totally sure and the only way I can test out my theory is to bring the frillio to him. Either way we may well need its healing properties at some point. I shall stay here on McDragon's rocks as long as you are on Harris."

"He couldn't sense anything from it when he touched it before."

"No, I know, but it's best to double check."

"Anyhow, Effel, how did you know I was here and that Biffy was as well?"

"I had a vision about it and it seemed to be quite a strong one which I couldn't ignore."

"Thank you Effel. That is amazing of you particularly as it is a very long way for you to come when you're not used to flying!"

She tilted her head to one side and he felt that if she'd been human she would have smiled.

It seemed to be a good time to find out if she knew anything about the swannees. Fishing it out of his pocket he showed her the piece of swannee Biffy had found by the dragon rocks. After examining it quite carefully Effel announced that it was something she was not familiar with, apart from the one time when one had secured the parcel that was delivered to Seraphina's hideaway. She had no idea if they could be found anywhere other than McMuran's island. She seemed to concur with Peter's gut feeling that it probably was something that only occurred in the magic dome.

It felt good to know that he now had a dragon for company. He would have to find ways to avoid Biffy so that he could get to spend time with her. Eventually he left her, rather reluctantly, so that she could try to regain some of the strength she had used up on her long flight.

CHAPTER TWELVE

It was a contented boy who trudged back to the house and he was even happier when he found his dad frying slices of the black pudding from Tarbert along with some fried eggs.

Biffy's yawn as he came through the kitchen door could have swallowed them all up it was so big. He reached up and stretched his arms above his head at the same time and then stared at the frying pan.

"What's that?" he asked peering more closely at it.

"Black pudding and I think you'll like it. It's a Scottish speciality." replied Peter's dad.

"What's in it?"

"Best not to ask," was the answer, "as it may put you off. But it's delicious."

"I like it with lots of tomato sauce as well," chipped in Peter.

His dad was quite right, Biffy did like the black pudding and then he followed it down with lots of slices of toast and marmalade. No wonder he was such a big boy.

After their breakfast they were encouraged to go

down to the beach and scout about so that dad could get on with some work. He mentioned that he was planning on trying to contact Mr McMuran and arrange a time to pick up whatever it was he'd left on the island during their previous trip.

Peter desperately wanted to be able to go to the island with his dad so he could look about and see if there were any more clues that might lead them to finding McDragon but he knew that would be risky and that he had to keep out of McMuran's way. Their last meeting had not been a good one, to say the least. McMuran had tried to kill him with wizard's fire.

He and Biffy put on their wellies and coats and walked down to the sea which was lapping gently onto the stony beach. The tide was in quite a way and the water was hiding the green colours which were at the lower part of McDragon's rocks. You could only see the yellow lichen which looked like gold but unusually the rock underneath was a pale grey. Usually it was very black. Peter guessed that Effel had made use of the rocks that usually hid McDragon as a cover for her big frame. They did look a slightly different formation than when McDragon was in position.

They climbed over the rocks onto the next little beach and peered into the various rock pools dotted about. Peter was able to show Biffy the mussels which clung to the seaweed and told him about when they had picked the cleanest ones and cooked them and how delicious they were.

"It smells a bit odd here, almost animally but very strange. Not something I have smelt before on a beach," Biffy commented.

"Yes dragony!" was Peter's response to him without thinking.

"You would say that Dragon boy!" Biffy laughed.

Effel had shielded herself from view on McDragon's rocks, but Peter could smell her strong scent – she was much whiffier than McDragon. "It must be something to do with her age," he mused.

The frillio, however, was sitting quite proudly near the rocks, out in open view.

"Wow, look at that, we saw one of those on our trip, do you remember? What did you say it was called?"

"A frillio. It feels very nice if you put your hand into it."

Peter watched with bated breath as Biffy pushed his fingers into the centre of the pink frillio.

"Are you sure you can feel something? I can't," and as before when Biffy removed his hand from the frillio and held it out in front of him it was a normal colour. There was no pinkness there.

Peter just shrugged and replied, "Maybe it only works on cold hands or something like that!"

"Well, I do get a little strange tingly feeling but I wouldn't describe it as nice."

"No matter, shall we collect some mussels and see if dad will cook them for dinner?"

That kept them occupied for an hour or so as they tried to find the biggest and cleanest mussels clinging to the seaweed on the rocks where the burn trickled into the sea. They had to peer underneath the strands of seaweed to find the best ones.

"I found some oysters once as well, but not on this beach," Peter told Biffy rather proudly.

"Dad liked them." Biffy looked rather amazed at that.

"Perhaps dad can arrange for us to go fishing while we are here. Do you like fishing Biffy?"

"Never done it before."

"Neither had I until we were here last time. We caught a lot of mackerel and it tastes even yummier if you've caught it yourself. I don't usually like fish much but it was so different to what we have had at home. I suppose it is because it is so very fresh. Where do you normally go on holiday?"

"Costa Brava usually on an eat and drink as much as you like holiday. Dad certainly drinks as much as he likes and my sister and I just try and keep out of the way as much as possible. He's really horrid and difficult when he's had a few drinks, just like he was when you saw him the other day."

Peter really didn't know what to say to that.

"We've never been on a holiday like this one. This is a really cool place to be!"

"I think so too. I didn't want to come here when mum first mentioned it because I thought it would be boring but I love it now. There's always something to do, even if it's just clambering around the beach and the rock pools."

"You're lucky, Dragon boy, I like the way your dad talks to you. Mine doesn't talk, he usually shouts. I don't think he likes me at all. He's a bit better with my sister – at least he doesn't hit her." Biffy looked down at his feet and Peter wondered if he was about to cry.

"Maybe your dad's unhappy about something and he takes it out on you. Is that why you used to bully me at school?"

"Could be I suppose. I've never really thought about it before. Wasn't a nice thing to do, was it?"

"No, you made going to school a horrible time for me!"

"I guess I was jealous. I used to watch you and either your mum or dad would bring you to school with your sister and give you a kiss or hug goodbye. Neither my mum or dad ever did that for us, we always had to walk on our own even when we were little, and sometimes the big boys would pick on us."

"Do you think we have enough mussels now?" Peter thought it time to change the subject, he didn't want Biffy to ask how the magical blast that Spit had made happen, which had knocked the bully gang for six, came about.

Peter's dad was quite pleased when he saw they'd picked so many mussels and he said he would make a nice dinner with them. The three of them cleaned the mussels and then cooked their supper together. There was a lot of laughter while they did it and the boys enjoyed their meal so much more having prepared it themselves.

CHAPTER THIRTEEN

The following morning Peter was up and about early as he usually was in Harris so he could nip over to see Effel before Biffy got up. He was washed and out of the door in a flash and down on the beach where he disturbed the otter having its breakfast on a nearby rock.

"Sorry!" he called out to it as he passed.

Effel was waiting for him, standing by the side of McDragon's rocks. She gave a very dragony smile when she saw him. It could have been mistaken for a grimace if he hadn't spent so much time with the other dragons before this. He realised that she was missing a few of her very long teeth, all of which were a bit green and stained. Her breath smelt pretty gross so he had to keep taking deep breaths in when his head was turned away and then let the air out very slowly.

"Did you see Biffy yesterday with the frillio, Effel?"

"Yes, Petersmith. It's just as I thought, he can sense and feel magic but it doesn't touch him at all. That is a good thing for you."

"I was wondering how Spit's magic blast altered Biffy

the way it has in view of the fact that you say he is non-magical."

"It's possible it made a difference because it was double or triple dragon magic which was channelled through you, as dragon kin. Spit was probably aided by Seraphina and Haribald."

"That kind of makes sense." They both pondered on that for a while.

"Are you feeling back to normal now Effel after your long flight?"

"Yes, thank you, Petersmith. I am much recovered. I will go and hunt fish shortly and that will help me stock up some more energy. What are your plans for today?"

"Well, that was what I needed to tell you, we're going to McMuran's island. Dad arranged with someone at the house that his papers would be left for him there. Biffy and I are to stay in the boat while he collects them."

"Good, if that man, McMuran, was going to be near you I would have had to have flown to the island to make sure you were kept safe. Seeing as I'm not needed to keep an eye on you two I will go to the seers' cave to check all the etchings there. It's been an age since I last did that!"

"Isn't that a bit far for you if you are a little jaded?"

"That's nothing laddie, even for a dragon as old as me!"

"Is it right what McDragon told me in that different pictures are shown to each dragon when they visit the caves? We wanted to find out what Spit's story was, but McDragon seemed to think that Spit would need to be able to fly there himself."

"That indeed is very true, Petersmith."

Peter glanced at his watch as he said "I must fly Effel!

Sorry, that means I must be off before dad notices I'm missing. Thank you for being our guard!" and he reached across holding his breath to avoid the bad fumes and gave her a kiss on her long nose.

If she was a human she would have blushed, "My pleasure. Let us hope we are successful in finding McDragon!"

"Yes. That is very important! Do be careful of the squawkins Effel, they seem to patrol near the seers' cave!"

"I'll certainly look out for them Petersmith. I'll see you later maybe."

* * *

On the big speedboat which was taking them to the island Peter and Biffy sat outside on the deck breathing in the cold air. It helped with any sea sickness they might feel. The sea spray from where the prow of the boat broke the waves lightly splashed them. It was a lovely bracing feeling and Peter was pleased to see that Biffy appeared to be enjoying it as well. He was proud to point out the stacks as they passed them where they watched hundreds of gannets diving and bringing up fish to eat. There were also tiny puffins flying hither and thither, settling on top of the rippling water. Biffy was entranced to see so many busy birds, it was definitely an eye opener for him.

"Fabulous! So fabulous! I guess not many people get to see that!"

They finally chugged slowly into the small stone harbour.

"Dad, I know you won't be long but can I take Biffy

round to the small beach that Mr McMuran sent me to last time I was here with you? We can stretch our legs a bit that way."

"Ok, go straight there and come back within about half an hour. As you know, it's quite a trek up those stone steps, so I'll have to stop a couple of times, but I plan to be as quick as I possibly can."

The seamen steadied each of them as they stepped from the boat to the stone jetty. They definitely needed that helping hand as they were all a little wobbly on their sea legs.

"This way Biffy!" Peter led Biffy up the stony steps and then across to where they could clamber down to the little beach. The last time Peter had been here had been when McDragon landed so that Peter could dismount to enable him to get on with his urgent mission of rescuing Seraphina's Pearl, which the wizard McMuran had stolen. It was on the verge of hatching and they needed to get it away in case the dragonite inside bonded with McMuran. That would have been a disaster. They also intended to rescue Spit, who was trapped inside the dome and couldn't get through the gossamer magical boundary. They'd had, and still had, no idea how Spit had ended up there. It was a mystery which they all hoped the dragon seers' cave might have answers to.

Considering it was some time since McDragon had landed here Peter was very surprised to see that the little beach still had the dips and gouges left by the huge dragon. He would have expected the sea to have filled the holes in, but maybe it was a more sheltered spot than he realised. It didn't matter anyway because no-one would guess the ruts were caused by dragon's talons. There was no sign of any more recent landing by McDragon, which was the real reason Peter had wanted to come to the beach now.

The boys mooched about and watched the birds that were flying over the sea and frequently diving into its depths for fish. Once the allotted time was nearly up, they scampered back across to the harbour in time to be helped back on board by the seamen. They timed it just right because Peter's dad appeared at the bottom of the steep steps just a few minutes after them. He was a little out of breath – it was a long trek down from the top.

"Good boys, I'm glad I didn't have to come and look for you. As we knew, Mr McMuran wasn't there but whoever I spoke to left the papers wrapped up in the porch for me as agreed. I was a little concerned they might have forgotten and it would have been an expensive wasted journey." He showed the package to the lads briefly, "I need these if I am to continue with my research into the island's history."

At that moment, one of the seamen gave a shout and pointed out to sea. They all rushed to the side of the boat, which was just pulling out of the harbour. There were two porpoises swimming in tandem, their fins showing above the surface of the sea as they arced up and over and then disappeared below the waves.

"Wow, look at that! That's something else!" Biffy stood staring with his mouth open in amazement. Peter felt exactly the same – he'd never seen porpoises before either.

The thought of the trip back seemed rather dull after the porpoises had left them. The mammals had swum alongside the boat for quite a while. Biffy said he thought there could be nothing to match the sight of two porpoises at such close quarters, although Peter secretly thought that perhaps dragons would be even more exciting.

Peter saw that the captain and Peter's dad were chatting and it turned out that there was an interesting cave further round the island which they couldn't see from where they had approached the harbour. From past experience, Peter knew that the island was narrow at each end with long stretches of cliffs along the sides and was much bigger than it actually appeared. It was agreed that they could do a small detour so they could have a look at the cave, but firstly the speedboat was manoeuvred slowly close in to the cliffs to enable them to watch the seabirds ducking and diving down from their nests high above them.

Shortly after that they zoomed along towards the northern part of the island. Hidden at the very end the boys could see they were chugging towards a slender gap where the cliff met the sea. With a very accomplished hand at the wheel the skipper turned the boat round so that he could reverse into the cavern. Peter thought that was very clever driving, not that that was the correct word for it he realised. Once inside there were some amazing stalactites hanging downwards from the ceiling of the cave, their colours ranging from grey to a beautiful turquoise blue. They were told that these had been here for hundreds of years and were forever changing as seawater dripped down them. The speedboat was reversed slowly back so that they could see more fissures in the cave's walls.

Biffy nudged Peter and whispered into his ear, "What's that Dragon boy? Can you see them?"

Peter had been looking the other way and when he turned he shuddered involuntarily, it looked like there were two gargoyle-like faces grinning at them from either side of one of the bigger black deep gouges in the walls and a little further back were some wide steps leading off behind them.

"Really, Biffy, what is it you're looking at?"

"There, either side of the blackness! It's like two ugly faces looking out at us, in fact they look rather like the gargoyles you sometimes see on the top of buildings."

Peter forced a laugh, "I suppose you could say that! Very strange," and he pretended to dismiss Biffy's comment, but now they were further back he felt that strange tingling in the back of his neck that always occurred when magic was about. He noticed that Biffy was rubbing the back of his neck thoughtfully while still staring at the faces in the wall.

"Seen enough boys?" asked Peter's dad.

"Yes, thanks dad. That was brilliant – something amazing to remember." Peter pulled his camera out of his pocket and snapped aimlessly around the cavern making sure he focussed a couple of times on the gargoyles. The flash automatically lit up the gloom in the cavern, however he wasn't sure if the pictures would come out. When he'd tried to take photos of McDragon in the past the big dragon had not appeared in them at all.

As the boat moved slowly forward Peter looked back over his shoulder – he felt sure that the gargoyle on the left lifted its lips in a snarl making him nearly jump in fright. The second one stared stonily at him, a nasty glare on its face and then it winked. Very scary! Luckily Biffy was too absorbed in watching the captain's skill at manoeuvring them out of the cave to notice.

CHAPTER FOURTEEN

As the Isle of Harris came into view on the horizon, the rocking of the boat sent Biffy off to sleep. His head kept nodding down onto his chest and then he would moan and sit up again, only to have his chin bouncing off his chest again a few moments later. His hands were tucked into his pockets to keep them warm and Peter studied him as he slumbered. It was very strange that he was now spending time with a boy who had bullied him mercilessly for many months in the past. That side of Biffy had not shown its head at all while they had been in Scotland. Was he likely to appear again or had Biffy learnt his lesson for good?

Once the engines slowed the boat's motion changed. Biffy woke with a little groan, and shook himself. He peered around him looking a bit disorientated.

"Well Dragon boy, you seem to have affected me somehow, I dreamt of a small dragon while I slept and he kept telling me excitedly that he was learning to fly. He told me over and over again. Very strange dream, I must say!"

Peter smiled as he realised Spit must be having flying lessons.

"What do you know Biffy, Scotland must be doing something to your brain cells."

* * *

They were back on Harris in time for a very late lunch of baps as usual. Then Peter's dad shooed them out into the fresh air as he wanted to concentrate on reviewing the papers he'd collected from the island.

Peter and Biffy went past McDragon's rocks, where Peter noticed that Effel was not in residence. He guessed she must have flown up to the seers' cave as she had said she would and he just hoped she'd had the sense to look out for the nasty squawkins.

Once they reached the next little beach as the tide was out quite a distance they started hunting for the cockle shells which often littered the surface of the beach. Peter produced a plastic bag out of his pocket so they could put their booty into it. It was fun being hunter gatherers and it wasn't long before the bag was feeling quite heavy. The most exciting find was a couple of oysters which they discovered when they paddled in the very cold water. Dad would love them!

While they were there Peter spotted an unknown bird flying high above them and he snatched up his binoculars, which were nearly always with him, and stared up at it.

"It's an eagle! Have a look Biffy! I'm sure it's an eagle up there!" Biffy scampered over to him and accepted the offer of looking through the binoculars. His face was a picture as he zoomed in on it.

"That's so very amazing! I've never ever seen one of those before!"

Peter didn't like to admit that he'd seen a couple of them before when McDragon had flown him up high to the dragon seers' cave but he'd never seen one from the ground.

Once the eagle disappeared off into the distance they resumed their scavenging and as he scrabbled about in the sea Peter's mind wandered to the cave where the gargoyle faces had been. What were they guarding? How could he find out?

There was a loud squawk very close to him, which made him jump.

"Archie, where have you been? I didn't see you yesterday. Have you been with Effel?"

The big black bird with the white streak down one wing squawked again and Peter had to assume that this was a yes.

"Is she OK?"

Another squawk. Archie didn't seem to look flustered at all so Peter guessed this meant there was nothing awry with her.

"Did she go to the seers' cave?"

The answer, again appeared to be yes. Speaking to a crow was such hard work and very one-sided!

"Are you talking to a bird? You're definitely mad!" called Biffy to him. It was lucky he was doing his scavenging far enough away not to be able to hear the questions Peter had been asking.

"He was here last time and I called him Archie. He seems quite tame you know."

"Really!" Biffy sounded amused. "You'll be speaking to dragons next!" and he burst in to laughter at the thought.

Archie flew off to perch on a nearby rock and watched them.

Eventually Peter and Biffy decided they'd found enough cockles and feeling quite content with their afternoon's work sat down next to one another to watch the sea while eating some chocolate which Peter had brought out with him.

Peter decided that now was a good time to broach the subject that had been bothering him for a while.

"Biffy, you seem to be a nice guy deep down and I know you said you were jealous of me but I still can't understand what on earth made you do those horrible things that you did to me at school? What did I do to deserve that sort of treatment?"

Biffy looked shamefacedly at the rocks below his feet as he shuffled about uncomfortably on his bottom.

"I dunno really. It was like the power of having a gang went to my head a bit. They seemed to look up to me when I was being such a bad guy. I'm really sorry, Dragon boy, I won't be doing it again, I can promise you that, not to you nor anyone else! I know I made your life hell for quite a time."

"That's an understatement if ever there was one! You know more people would look up to you if you showed what you are really like inside. I don't have many friends because most of the other kids were scared of you and you don't have any friends either do you? Just those cronies of yours who are in your gang."

"I don't have a gang anymore. Something happened

that first day back at school. I can't quite remember what it was, but I know it gave me a big shock. I keep trying to fathom out what happened – do you know?"

Peter just shrugged his shoulders, he wasn't going to lie and he wasn't going to give out any information about Spit either. He'd made a promise to the dragons.

Silence reigned for a while and then they decided to go inside to see what was occurring about dinner and if they could have the cockles.

Peter's dad was really delighted to see the oysters and he suggested they had cockles and spaghetti for dinner. Biffy volunteered to help with the preparation while Peter laid the table and then read a book he had brought with him on birds. There were no crows in the pictures that had a white streak on one of their wings and Spit had told Peter that this had made the big bird an outcast with other crows. As far as Peter and Spit were concerned it was the other crows' loss and their gain.

CHAPTER FIFTEEN

Again, Peter was up early and despite the rain he shot down across the beach to see if Effel was back. She didn't bother emerging out of McDragon's rocks because, she explained, it had been more tiring than she had anticipated flying to the dragon seers' cave but she was very happy to talk to him nevertheless. Archie flew over and hopped up and down the rocks to listen to them.

"What did you find at the seers' cave, Effel?"

"Not very much that was helpful Petersmith, I'm afraid. There seems to be some kind of magic fogging anything to do with McDragon and that has affected not only myself but also the other dragon seers."

"Oh no, I was so hoping there would be some clue or other there!"

"So was I. There is an illustration of you meeting with me, and then one of us on the island with Seraphina, Haribald, Spit and a sick Popple. After that, the squawkins' arrival with the package, but as I was there with you that would be clear to me. I passed other etchings which I could not understand, but there is also a picture of you with Popple but that is a total mystery to me. You appear to be lying down and Popple has something stripy in front of her so I cannot see her clearly. Who knows why! I could be mistaken, but I didn't feel that you were on Seraphina's hideaway island because the backdrop to the picture is very dark rocks. Biffy is alone in one of the pictures holding something rather like a stick. I'm sure it will all make sense when the time comes. These were not my visions but belonged to another dragon seer so they are alien to me."

"Bother!" was all that Peter could think to say and then his stomach started to rumble. He was hungry.

"I'll go back for my breakfast and we can both have a think about what our next move should be. I'm very worried because there is not a lot of time before we have to go home." As he turned to go he then looked back at the rocks, "By the way, when we were at McMuran's island the captain of the boat took us round to see a beautiful cave on the opposite side to where I used to enter the magic dome and, well it was Biffy who pointed them out, there were two gargoyle-like rocks either side of a deep fissure at the back of the cave. I could have sworn one of them winked at me! I wouldn't have noticed them but for Biffy. They made my neck prickle and Biffy was rubbing his neck too."

"I'm sure that boy will help you somehow. Try and keep him close to you."

"OK Effel," his stomach rumbled again, "I'm always hungry here!" and he ran back to the cottage.

His dad was inside cooking some bacon to go into sandwiches.

"You're up early my boy!"

"Yes, I have to make the most of being here – I just love it!"

His dad just smiled, Peter's response pleased him immensely.

Biffy staggered down the stairs slowly and was rubbing his eyes as he came into the little kitchen diner.

"Can I smell breakfast? Oh, lovely, bacon! I'm hungry! What is it about being here that makes me so hungry?"

"I think it's the fresh air Biffy, I'm always hungry too." Peter smiled at the other boy. Then he looked at Biffy a bit harder and leant in close to whisper, "You don't look so good, couldn't you sleep?"

"I had some strange dreams Dragon boy which kept me awake." Biffy whispered back. "I dreamt of that small dragon again, but this time he was shouting over and over again, "They took Popple! They took Popple!" and every time I fell asleep the voice kept reverberating in my head. It was very, very strange! The dragon looked rather battered and had deep gouges down his front. What do you make of that Dragon boy? What do you think a Popple is? And there was another word… squats or something like that. Fancy a dragon speaking like that! It must be something in the air here!"

Peter shrugged nonchalantly while inside he was panicking. Biffy must have been sleeping with the dragon scale in his hand. What could he do? A promise to a dragon is an important thing to keep and until he was released from his oath he couldn't talk to Biffy about it and anyway, why on earth would he believe Peter?

There was silence for a while apart from the sound of chewing and slurping at cups of tea. All of the time Peter was trying to plan how he was going to get down to see Effel again. What's more it had to be very, very soon.

* * *

It was an amazing piece of luck really. Peter's dad said he'd arranged to take them fishing later on that day but first he needed to press on with the work he'd started the day before. Biffy opted to go up to his room for a short while before joining Peter on the beach.

As soon as the coast was clear Peter sped across the shingle as fast as his legs would carry him and skidded to a halt near to where Effel was using McDragon's rocks as her hideaway.

He started calling as soon as he was close enough and she must have heard the panic in his voice because immediately the rocks started to melt away from her body and it wasn't long before she was standing before him in all her holey glory.

"Petersmith! Where's the fire?"

"Effel! Effel! Biffy had dreams last night and they were all of Spit shouting that "they" had taken Popple. Then he mentioned squats, but I think he meant squawkins! Spit looks quite injured. What should we do? I guess Biffy must have fallen asleep holding on to the scale."

"Petersmith, that is terrible news. I think firstly I need to go to Seraphina's island and find out exactly what has happened. If Biffy is correct and the squawkins have taken Popple then presumably she is where McDragon is." She nodded her big head thoughtfully as she pondered on the problem. "Yes, I am positive that is what we need to do before we go off half-cocked on a rescue mission. Please go and get the frillio Petersmith, we may need its healing powers. You will have to come with me in dragon time because I will need your help navigating there. I will warm you so that we can fly without you freezing."

Doing as he was instructed Peter went to collect the frillio from it resting place, which was exactly where he and Biffy had last seen it. It was only a short way away from Effel, and tucking it safely inside his coat, he felt yet again that lovely soothing feeling which it always gave him. As he returned to the dragon's side there was a loud cawing from the rocks behind him and then a rush of wings as Archie landed on his shoulder. He must have heard the whole conversation and decided to come along too. Spit and he were firm friends after they'd met in McMuran's magical dome, a long time before Peter had arrived there.

Effel snorted heat over the lad before he struggled to clamber aboard, his dodgy hand hampering him somewhat. She used her snout to try and push him upwards, much like McDragon used to have to do. As soon as he was in position, her scales locked down on his knees and held him safe. Now was the tricky part – she had to take off and there was only a very small drop from the rocks she was standing on and then the incredibly cold sea.

Peter held on tightly to the floppy spine in front of him – he wasn't looking forward to this at all. Although her taking off and landing skills were improving they were still not that good, to say the least! Effel flapped her tattered wings, up and down, up and down, faster and faster. Archie decided it might be a lot safer for him to be up in the air on his own so he left Peter's shoulder and hovered above them. The big wings gathered speed and then with a final jolt Effel launched herself from the rocks and immediately splashed down into the bitterly cold sea. Fortunately, it was not too deep and Peter had sensibly bent his legs at the knees and lifted his feet up as far as he could behind him. His grip on the neck scale tightened keeping him relatively safely anchored on board. She must have touched the rocky bottom with her feet because he could feel her legs pushing against the water to try and propel herself forwards.

The old dragon persevered and carried on beating her wings and then bracing her whole body, managed to give a leap upwards. It wasn't enough so she tried again and again and finally, although it wasn't an elegant jump it seemed to do the trick and there was just one big splash and they took off, her tummy grazing the top of the water. For quite a while she flew very low but at least they were airborne, although it was touch and go as to whether she kept them above the waves or dipped down into the sea. Peter could feel the humungous effort she was making. A gust of wind suddenly blew from behind them and that helped the old dragon gain a little more height. As before, it was a very bumpy ride and Peter wondered if he ought to buy himself some seasickness pills so that he could take one before his next flight with her. He bet that amazing shop that sold everything in Tarbert would have some. He kept his mind off the bouncy ride by trying to remember what the shop had been called. It began with "A", he knew that.

Archie flew alongside them and at long last, Peter

thought it would be safe enough to drop his feet back into the position they usually were when he rode a dragon, which was much the same as if he had been riding a horse. He gave a sigh of relief it hadn't been very comfortable sitting like that.

"Well done Effel! That was really tough for you, wasn't it?"

"Too true, Petersmith. Too true. It's hard enough flying as it is, but then your added weight doesn't help. What's more I am still a little tired from my journey yesterday to the seers' cave."

"Well, Archie and I will be on guard for squawkins so they don't take us by surprise!"

Archie cawed his agreement to this. He most definitely didn't want to become fodder for a squawkin.

Peter looked back towards the island they had just left and he thought he spied a lone figure on the beach looking across the sea at them.

"Whew! It's lucky we left when we did Effel, because I think I can see Biffy back there near McDragon's rocks, or should I call them Effel's rocks for now?"

All Peter heard was a "Hrummpf!" from the dragon. She was concentrating hard.

They flew for what seemed like an age. Peter could feel Effel was beginning to really labour to keep them just a few feet above the waves. Her chest was heaving in and out so badly that he could feel it pushing on his legs. He looked around them, searching for something to help. Then he spotted a tiny island with rocky stacks towering up out of the sea.

"Effel!" he shouted at her, "what if you fly to the top of

the tall rocks over there and have a rest for a short while to get your breath?"

She didn't even have the strength to answer him but he could feel her fighting to gradually lift them higher and higher until she eventually came to a stop, perched very precariously on top of the narrow stacks. Seabirds squawked as they scattered in fright. She plonked herself down and lay her knobbly chin down on the bird poo coloured rock in front of her. Fortunately there was just enough room for her on the top.

"Shall I get down Effel? Will that help?" although secretly he was hoping she would say no because he rather thought it might be very slippery on the slimy rocks due to all the seabird poo. It smelt pretty awful too.

"It's OK Petersmith. Wait there for a while. It was good thinking on your part to come up here and I should get my breath back soon, I hope."

There was silence between them although the screeching of the furious gulls and gannets made up for it. Every now and then one of them would zoom down towards them to try and scare them from the craggy top and when Peter wasn't pinching his nose to stop inhaling the very strong smell of bird muck which was overwhelming him, he was waving his arms about like windmills to stop the birds dive bombing him. Luckily most of them were too frightened of the huge dragon or they might have joined forces and mobbed the two of them, trying to push them off of their resting place. Archie, rather sensibly, had flown down and Peter opened his jacket so the big bird could hide next to the frillio. He most definitely didn't want to be attacked by a hoard of angry birds.

"Effel, might the frillio help you to recover?"

"Good thinking Petersmith, you are definitely dragon kin. Can you pass it to me please?"

Peter rummaged around inside his coat, moving Archie over as he took a gentle grip on the frillio. Effel bent her long neck back towards him so that he could lean over and place it in her maw. She kept her mouth open and turned back to place it carefully between her front legs and then rested her huge head on top of it, squashing it. As she did Peter could feel her shuddering breath beginning to slow down as she relaxed and eventually a loud snore echoed around them sending yet more frightened birds up into the air. Peter let her sleep. It was the only way they would get to their destination safely. He kept a close lookout while alternating between ducking low to avoid being pecked at by the gulls which kept swooping down at them and waving his arms about which were beginning to get very tired.

After a time Effel finally raised her head when a passing bird was brave enough to give a nasty peck on the end of her nose. She jerked her head up angrily and growled menacingly at her attacker. Rather sensibly it flew away.

"Petersmith, we can continue with our journey, I think. Hopefully that will have been enough of a rest for me."

"Effel, have you eaten since you got back from your trip to the seers' cave?"

"No, Petersmith, I just needed to sleep. That's what happens when you are as old as the hills, like I am."

"Well, I think in future you should always make sure

you eat because if you don't, where will you get your energy from when you need it?"

"Good point, laddie. The trouble is that since I became a dragon seer I haven't needed much fuelling. I will remember in future. Now let's be away!" She returned the frillio to him and then waved her wings majestically up and down before leaping from the top of the guano covered rocks. The gulls gave chase, pretending they were seeing her off and Peter gave a sigh of relief, it was so good to be away from that smothering disgusting smell. He moved his shoulders about as they were aching from all the movement his arms had had to make.

This time because they started from a good height it meant she could use the air currents to speed their passage.

CHAPTER SIXTEEN

At long last they began their descent down towards Seraphina's island hideaway. Effel trumpeted loudly to let the dragons know of her arrival and Peter could see Spit jumping about down below. Their landing was worse than before and Effel ended up collapsing onto her belly and skidding along until she crashed into the rocks. Peter held on for dear life wishing he had a seatbelt as he pressed himself down onto her neck trying to avoid the sharp points of the neck scales that weren't floppy. Once she had come to a halt, Effel stayed in that flat position panting loudly.

"Petersmith!" Spit shouted loudly, "I am so pleased to see you!"

As soon as the scales over his knees released him Peter slithered down to the ground.

"How do you do Spit?"

"Not very well Petersmith! Not well at all! How do you do?"

"I've been better Spit. I've been very worried about you all, and particularly Popple. What has happened?"

Spit started to hum the dragon song and Effel, with her head still on the ground, hummed in reply. Then she raised her now battered face and shook her whole body, turning to peer at Spit.

"Yes, what has happened? Where are Seraphina and Haribald?"

"They are away trying to find a trace of Popple. The squawkins took her! They took my little Popple!" Tears began to pour down the little dragon's face.

"There, there, Spit! Calm yourself and tell us what happened?"

"Well, Popple and I were out playing just over there," and he nodded his head over to a small clearing at the edge of the rocks. "Out of nowhere the squawkins shot down from the sky. There was no warning at all because they didn't make a sound, not like they usually do. One snatched Popple up and carried her off. I leapt after it and tried to bring it down but the other squawkin attacked me. Seraphina and Haribald were a little way off catching fish and they raced over once they realised what had happened, but it was too late. They followed in pursuit but they still haven't returned and that was yesterday. I've been here all alone since then, worrying." More huge dragon tears flooded down his face. He was quite distraught.

"Oh, poor Spit!" Peter gave him a friendly pat on the neck trying to comfort his friend. "We thought something had happened like that. You did so well by managing to get a message through to Biffy. That was brilliant of you." Spit brightened up a little bit at the praise as Peter continued, "Biffy told me about his dream, although he

83

didn't understand it at all. Once I'd related it to Effel she said we had to come."

"I'm so happy to see you both. So pleased! I had no idea what to do! I still cannot fly for very long."

Spit looked a sad sight. He had deep gouges down his face and neck and particularly across the patch where Peter had taken scales from over his chest area so that they could use one to talk to each other. It was apparent that the squawkin which attacked him had realised that was a weak area.

"Spit, you need to heal the cuts you can reach. They could go septic and then you'll be in a really bad way. Go on! Do it now!" Peter instructed his friend.

"I'll do the ones you cannot reach," Effel told him as she struggled to her feet.

There was a lot of hissing and a nasty burning smell as Spit began to heal his cuts. Effel dribbled over the ones which were too high up for him to reach, being very gentle around his face area. Once he was looking more like his old self, he reciprocated and helped Effel heal the wounds she had sustained from her erratic landing.

Dragon gunge is just amazing, much better than plasters and Spit was left with only a few small scars on his chest area which Peter told him made him look very fierce, much like Effel. Spit started dancing about when he heard that.

"What shall we do Petersmith and Seer Effel?"

Effel was still looking rather exhausted so Peter replied, "I think Effel needs to rest for a few minutes Spit. Our journey has taken its toll of her. Shall we leave you Effel, for a short while?"

"Yes, please Petersmith. I will be well again in no time at all, I am sure!" Peter wasn't so sure but he led Spit away in the hope she would sleep.

"Petersmith! Let me show you my flying! Look at this!" and without more ado Spit launched himself from the top of the nearby rocks and started gliding down towards the sea. There were only a few small waves there as Spit flattened his wings against his sides and straightened himself up so he was like an arrow as he dived into the dark water. Peter held his breath as he watched his friend, whose actions were very reminiscent of the gannets. Shortly afterwards Spit reappeared, bobbing about on top of the surface for a moment, then he stretched his wings and flapped them up and down. Water sprayed out either side of him and almost effortlessly he was suddenly climbing back up into the air towards where Peter was standing. Peter's thought at that moment was what a shame Effel wasn't in a condition to take off like that anymore. When Spit landed lightly next to Peter he dropped something out of his mouth onto the ground.

"Wow! That's a big fish Spit!"

Spit looked down proudly at it.

"Err… Spit?"

"Mmmm." Spit looked as if he was about to gobble the fish down.

"I don't suppose you would offer the fish to Effel would you? I rather think that dragons don't do that usually but Effel hasn't eaten since yesterday when she flew all the way to the seers' cave. What would help her more than sleep, I believe, is if she could refuel."

Spit straightened up, looking very important.

"Of course, Petersmith! Of course! Seer Effel can have the fish and I will go and get her another one too! You take this one to her and I will see you in a minute. Seraphina says I am very good at catching fish." And he was gone in the blink of an eye.

Peter picked up the rather large fish and carried it over to Effel. Her long snout twitched and she opened one eye.

"Effel, Spit has caught this fish for you and he has flown off to go and get you another one too. I thought it might help you recover some of your strength."

"How thoughtful of you both, Petersmith. Yes, that will be very good for me." Her big head reached over to the fish and it was gulped down in one go. She belched – it was not a nice smell at all and Peter backed away. Then her head banged back onto the ground as her eye closed.

Peter returned to where he had been before and looked across the sea. No sign of Spit.

He waited.

Then the little dragon appeared on top of the sea as he had done before, water spraying everywhere before he flew back up to where Peter was standing. Another large fish was plopped onto the ground.

"I shall get her another one!" He was gone.

Effel managed to gobble down three large fish and was starting to look a little better. She was still flat out on the ground when Peter felt a tingling at the back of his neck.

"Effel! Effel! Something is happening, I can feel it, can you?" He looked out to sea where Spit had just disappeared under the water again. There was something travelling very fast bouncing across the waves as it came towards them.

"Effel! What is that?"

Effel groaned as she raised her head and peered into the distance.

"Oh no! Petersmith we must move to the safety of the rocks! Now!" and she staggered to her feet and wobbled about dangerously.

"But what about Spit?!"

"We can do nothing for the moment, Petersmith! Run for your life!" Archie, who had been hopping around them hoping for some stray bits of fish, took off into the sky as Peter and Effel headed for the overhang where Popple had been when she was ill. They pressed themselves against the back wall, Effel's grey colour blending in nicely with the rocks behind them.

"Oh Effel! I do hope Spit will be OK!" Peter's voice wobbled. He was so scared for his friend. "What is it coming? It looks rather like a small tornado swirling round and round."

"It is something like that Petersmith but it has been made with magic. It is made up of terrible wind and water and if any of us get caught up in it we will spin and spin totally out of control. I guess it could gather us up and whisk us away to where it has come from. There was something like that in one of the etchings in the seers' cave but I didn't realise what it was and I cannot remember now what happened. If only I had paid more attention to it!"

Peter patted her tough old scales kindly, "You can't do everything Effel! You've done so much already!"

They both looked out over the sea and as they did they saw a dragon's head appear above the waves. The swirling mass of wind and water whipped round and round as it got closer and closer to Spit. At the same time a small black thing sped down out of the sky towards it and plunged itself into the deep centre. The spinning wind seemed to lose some of its speed. Spit ducked down under the water again suddenly aware that he was in terrible danger. Then the little black bird that was Archie was spat out and he plunged into the deep sea.

"Oh Archie! How brave! But he cannot swim – he's a crow not a gull!" cried Peter.

"That's what I saw in the cave, Petersmith. Archie either going into the magic tornado or being thrown out of it! I didn't realise it was Archie as it was just a black blob in the picture."

The swirling magic mass had slowed. Somehow Archie had managed to break its rhythm and finally it just stopped and died down into nothing.

Peter ran out for a better look at the sea.

"Careful Petersmith, we cannot be sure it will not start up again."

"Effel, the tingling has gone from the back of my neck so I think it is OK. But where, oh where, is Spit?"

They both scanned the sea hoping to spot the dragon, then Peter remembered he had a small pair of binoculars in his coat pocket and he dragged them out to peer frantically through them.

"Wow! Look at that! Isn't he amazing?"

Spit bobbed up and started his flight back towards them. He had what must be another fish in his mouth. He landed next to them, shaking himself hard to rid himself of the sea water that was running down his body. Then he gently deposited his booty down onto the ground.

It wasn't a fish, it was a black crow with a white stripe along its wing. Poor Archie looked lifeless and when Peter touched his chest he couldn't feel any heartbeat. He looked at Effel and shook his head sadly.

"Petersmith, get my frillio quickly!" Peter ran to the rock in the sunshine where he'd put the frillio when they'd arrived. "Now find the other frillio that Spit saved and brought here! Hurry my boy! If we have any chance to save Archie then you have to do it at the speed of light!"

One frillio was placed on top of Archie and the other one underneath so he was cushioned between them. Then they waited, very impatiently.

Spit looked forlorn. "What happened to Archie? What was it?"

"It was bad magic Spit… very bad magic. Archie saved you by diving into the whirlwind's core and it dispersed. It might have swept you up and spirited you away. That was incredibly brave of him. You are a very lucky dragon to have such a good friend!"

Spit's head drooped further down.

"Will he be OK? Is he going to live?"

"We have to wait and hope that the frillios work their own magic on him. I am not at all sure if we are too late to help him," answered Effel quietly, staring down at the soaking wet bird.

Peter couldn't speak at all, he was so choked up. This was the second time that they'd thought that Archie had died and each time it was because he was such a very brave bird.

They stood in a circle around the crow on his frillio cushion.

"Did I see something move Effel?"

"Not sure Petersmith." She answered gently, "I rather think not."

They continued their vigil in silence. Nothing happened. Peter couldn't take his eye off of the poor crow.

Suddenly there was a choking caw and the frillio on top of the bird slipped onto the ground. Archie's body was juddering and seawater spewed out of his beak. They waited with bated breath and amazingly, his chest started to move up and down and he struggled to his feet, wobbling about drunkenly.

"Archie!" shouted Spit, "You are saved! Thank my golly goodness!"

"You saved one another!" Peter told them relieved to find he could smile again. Spit started to bounce up and down, he looked very proud and happy. Archie cawed quietly, happy at being alive.

Effel gave the small dragon a little nudge. "Well done Spit and well done to you too Archie! How you survived that magic whirlwind I have no idea at all but what you did for your friend was amazing!"

Archie struggled to his feet and then hopped up onto Spit's scaly shoulder and gave his best friend a peck.

"Effel, do you think McMuran conjured up the whirlwind?"

"Quite likely, Petersmith. It's lucky your dragon kin magic kicked in and gave us a warning or else the tornado might have caught you instead. I rather think I would be too big for it."

Peter's tummy rumbled.

"Would you like me to catch you a fish Petersmith?" asked Spit.

"No thank you Spit! I'm supposed to be going fishing with my dad and Biffy when I get back."

CHAPTER SEVENTEEN

Effel decided it was time to return Petersmith back to Harris. The fish that Spit had brought her and her nap had done their job. As they prepared to leave she instructed Spit that he must somehow get a message to Petersmith via Biffy as soon as Seraphina and Haribald returned. She believed that they couldn't both have been captured, although how on earth McDragon had been taken remained a big mystery. Archie was staying with Spit to stop him fretting while he was on his own and, if it became necessary, Archie would make the long journey to find Effel who would be near McDragon's rocks, but they all hoped that wouldn't be necessary.

All that excitement was very tiring and Peter soon nodded off on the bouncy flight home. That was good on two counts, firstly because he couldn't feel the seasickness which generally accompanied a flight with Effel and, secondly, he wouldn't be too worn out to go fishing. On the downside, of course, was that he wouldn't be on the lookout for squawkins.

As they neared the cottage Peter spotted Biffy pacing up and down on the shore and Effel had to drop down low over the sea, which wasn't too great an effort for her, and land on the next little beach out of sight. As was her usual practice, she crashed down onto the shingle and slid along on her belly leaving huge gouges in the pebbles to show the soft sand underneath.

Peter dismounted quickly and scampered along, clambering over the rocks in the hope that he could creep up and surprise Biffy. Once close enough, he walked nonchalantly round the back of the cottage. Biffy immediately called out, "Where have you been? I've been searching and searching for you for ages!"

Peter tried not to look surprised but he remembered that for some reason dragon time didn't seem to work properly on Biffy.

"I've been mooching about, that's all."

Biffy looked very puzzled. "Well, lunch is ready and then we're going fishing."

"Great! I'm starving!" and Peter rushed into the house to avoid any more questions.

Biffy was right, a plate piled high with sandwiches was on the table. As usual Peter's adventures with the dragons had made him incredibly hungry and he stuffed the food into his mouth as fast as he could.

"Manners! Peter." His dad said fiercely. "Your mum would be very cross if she could see you eating like that. If you get indigestion it won't help you on the boat. You don't want to feed the fish do you?"

Peter grinned at him, "Sorry dad. You're right I don't want to be like Alice." Alice was always sick when she was on a boat.

After clearing up they set off on the trek to the car. Peter's legs were a little tired from his dragon ride but there was nothing else for it but to walk along as if he was feeling on top of the world. Biffy kept up with him but they couldn't talk much because Peter made sure he stayed fairly close to his dad. He took in a deep breath enjoying the salty smell of the seaweed and kelp on the beach just below them.

"Are we meeting Callum at the same place as before dad?"

"Yes, son, we are." He turned to smile at Biffy, "I hope you like fishing Biffy."

"I've never done it before sir, so I hope I can do it OK."

"It's a doddle Biffy." said Peter. "The fish almost jump into the boat! Let's hope we'll have nice fresh fish for tea."

Biffy seemed to have such a wonderful time on the boat fishing. He kept laughing and smiling, even when he was waiting for the fish to bite. Peter just kept glancing at him very surprised because he had never seen the other boy as relaxed and happy as he was. Yet again he wondered where Biffy the bully had gone.

They used the darrows that they'd bought on their previous trip. The darrow consisted of some small pieces of wood which were joined together to make up a square frame and the fishing line was wrapped round and round the frame. Pretty feathers and strips of shiny foil were attached to evil sharp hooks and were tied to the fishing line with a weight on the end of them to make sure the line would drop down in the water. The fish loved them and the boys kept feeling a tug on their lines and then would wind them up to see the bright glossy fish wiggling about on the hooks. The mackerel were supposed to be put into a bucket but quite often one would leap and end up on the floor of the small boat and at one point they had about six slippery fish skidding around their feet until Callum very kindly put each of them out of their misery with a bonk on the head. The bucket was full when they started heading homewards. Callum told them the fish were early this year due to the surprisingly warm weather they'd been having.

Peter's dad offered some of their catch to Callum, who only took a couple as he'd caught some fish the previous day. He suggested they stopped off on their way home at a tiny family run restaurant and possibly might be given a few pounds for them, so long as no-one else had beaten them to it. It was a shame to waste such beautiful fish.

As they sped along bouncing gently across the small waves, Peter suddenly felt a tingle in his neck. He rubbed it and looked round. Biffy was also having a rub of his neck. The sea was getting choppier and choppier and the boat began to rock from side to side as it tried to ride the waves.

"I wonder what's causing this?" called Callum, "The weather was supposed to be fine and calm today. Boys! You had better get into the cuddy so you don't fall in. Quickly now, in case it gets worse!"

The sky was still a lovely blue colour and there were no clouds. Peter moved carefully into the small covered in section at the front of the boat and set himself down next to Biffy.

"What's that there?" asked Biffy, pointing out of the window.

Callum looked puzzled, as did Peter's dad. "I can't see anything!"

Peter could and what's more he knew what it was! It was a whirlwind spinning its way across the sea towards them.

Biffy muttered to Peter, "Why can't they see it?"

"I don't know, but it doesn't look at all nice, does it?"

"Well at least you can see it too."

Peter's dad and Callum both sat down on the bench seat just outside the cuddy and hung on for dear life as the whirlwind battered the boat about. The bucket of mackerel slid about on the bottom, tipping some of their catch out onto the floor. The boat bounced and flounced around. At one point Peter let out a big yell as his head hit the roof of the cuddy. Biffy was flung across the seat and ended up the other side from where he had been sitting and Peter's dad and Callum were just trying to make sure they didn't fall overboard. They were all wearing life jackets but none of them wanted to end up in that freezing cold black sea.

Almost as suddenly as it started, the whirlwind swept away from them going back the way it had come. The sea started to become calmer and gradually everything was back to normal, almost as if it had never started.

"That was very strange." muttered Callum, "What on earth caused that to happen. Must have been some freak weather condition."

"It looked like some sort of whirlwind," Biffy called out.

"I didn't see anything like that, did you Callum?" Peter's dad asked.

"No, didn't notice anything at all. All very, very, odd. I'll have a chat to the people in the bar tonight to see if they experienced that and if they knew what it was. All these years at sea and I've never been caught out like that!"

Biffy and Peter just stared at one another. Then Biffy whispered in Peter's ear, "This morning when I couldn't find you, one of those wind things swept onto the beach, almost out of nowhere. There were pebbles flying everywhere and I had to duck right down between the rocks and hide my head in my arms. It seemed to circle round and round me and then went away. I almost felt it was looking for something or someone and couldn't find what it was searching for."

"That's odd, our bay is usually very calm and if the wind does come up all we see are a few white horses on top of the waves. It just gets choppy."

"Well, I got the itchy feeling at the back of my neck just like I did just before it came on us now."

Peter shivered inside. What was it looking for? He needed to talk to Effel, and very soon.

"Dragon boy, this is a strange place, lovely, but strange. Almost like there's magic here, and I have never believed in magic before this! What with the weird dreams of dragons and suchlike. What on earth is happening to me?!"

Peter looked away, he could explain it all but he wasn't allowed to.

* * *

The boys were thrilled to discover that the little family run restaurant wanted the mackerel and gave them some money for them – not a lot, but enough to buy a very small present for each of their mums if they wanted to. What's more they were told to bring any more fish that they caught to them.

Dinner was the gorgeous fried mackerel with lovely crispy skin and some chip like potatoes that Peter's dad had cooked in the oven and frozen peas. They then made some pancakes to have with sugar and lemon for pudding and that had caused a lot of laughter when they had a competition to see who could toss theirs the highest in the air and then catch them back in the frying pan. That was another new experience for Biffy – it seemed he had never done any cooking before apart from the small lessons they had at school. He said that at home they ate mainly burgers or sausages, chips and frozen food because his mum didn't have time to prepare food after she got in from work.

"Perhaps you should learn to cook Biffy," Peter's dad suggested. "Then you could help your mum out in the kitchen. Vegetables are quite easy to prepare and cook as well as being healthy."

Biffy smiled at the thought.

"I might just do that. Can I help you while we're here? I know there are only a few days left but I might learn something."

"Of course! We'll start tomorrow."

Just before they went to bed that night Callum rang to say that no-one in Tarbert had noticed any weather problems or reported any to the coast guard. It was going to remain a mystery.

Peter lay in bed and tried desperately hard to try and

stay awake so he could sneak down to see Effel. It was an impossibility and he soon slipped into a deep dreamless sleep, his exertions during the day finally taking their toll of him.

CHAPTER EIGHTEEN

Morning arrived and Peter stretched out in bed feeling well rested. Then he remembered he needed to get down to see Effel before Biffy and his dad got up, so he crept into the bathroom and brushed his teeth and tiptoed down the stairs trying to avoid the ones he knew creaked when you stood of them.

Effel was already waiting by the sea shore in her holey finery as he splashed through the shallows to get to McDragon's rocks.

"Petersmith, how are you today?"

"Okay Effel, but something very strange happened yesterday."

She tipped her head to one side to listen to him more closely.

He told her how Biffy had seen the whirlwind like tornado on the beach as if it were looking for someone and then also all about the one that bounced the boat about so dreadfully when they were fishing. He explained that no-one else on the water at the same time had been affected by the fierce sea.

"So, where were you Petersmith, when the whirlwind spun around the boat?"

"I was in the cuddy, which is the covered in bit of the boat. Biffy was with me."

She thought about it for a while, and while she did Peter listened to the lapping of the small waves on the sea shore and inhaled the lovely smell of the sea and seaweed. That ended abruptly when she turned to stare at him and he caught a whiff of her awful breath. It took a great effort for him not to step backwards away from the huge old dragon. It made him want to heave.

"Oh dear! I can only imagine that the whirlwind was looking for you, Petersmith! It obviously isn't Biffy, as it didn't bother him when you weren't there. You were only safe yesterday because you were inside the boat so it couldn't reach you."

That sounded really scary to Peter.

"What would it want with me?"

"I guess if the wind is made magically by McMuran then he needs you for some reason or other. Maybe something to do with McDragon or even Popple."

"I wonder how he found out I was on Harris?"

"Maybe the squawkins have seen you and reported back to him."

Peter was trying very hard to look brave – after all he was dragon kin. It wasn't easy though because inside he was feeling very shaky.

"Petersmith…"

"Yes, Effel."

"You must be very careful from now on. Keep a sharp eye out and keep that boy with you at all times. If you are taken he will help somehow, of that I am sure."

"But what will he do?"

"Petersmith, I have no idea. No idea at all. I have not had any visions of late which might help and the pictures in the dragon seers' cave were not really clear to me at all." She hesitated, "There was that picture of you with Popple though, but as I said I didn't know whether you were both on Seraphina's island or somewhere totally different." She stopped again, deep in thought.

"There is also the etching I told you about of Biffy on his own! Oh dear! You must be so alert Petersmith! Be on your guard at all times when you are out in the open air." Peter nodded slowly back at her as he absorbed what she was saying.

His thoughts were broken into when his tummy rumbled. It must be time for breakfast.

"I should go back now Effel, my stomach tells me that my breakfast must be ready soon. I'll be very careful and make sure I stay close to Biffy. It's strange, I don't seem to mind his company nowadays – he seems almost like a different boy to that horrible one that used to bully me at school."

"Maybe the dragon magic that Spit used on him changed him in more ways than intended Petersmith. Dragon magic can do amazing things."

Peter smiled at the memory of that day when Spit's dragon magic had somehow blasted all the school bullies to the ground. It had certainly done the trick! Biffy and his gang had left him alone after that.

He still needed to try and talk to Biffy about his dad hitting him. So far, they hadn't really had time to dwell on it at all and as Biffy had been enjoying himself so much it seemed a shame to bring up such a horrid subject and spoil his unexpected break.

He spotted the frillio not too far away and began to walk over to it. Effel called out urgently.

"Petersmith, be careful! Do you remember I told you that the frillio could be rather nasty when it begins to send up a flower spike. If you look carefully you'll see that there is a bud forming in the centre! Whatever you do, don't touch it!"

"I won't!" he called back studying the lovely pink thing looking so serene as it sat on the rocks. Sure enough, he could see a small bud right in the centre just as Effel had described.

"How long before the flower appears Effel?"

"Won't be long at all Petersmith. Frillios have a flower spike rather than a pretty flower and they only take a very short time to produce it. It's my belief that because a frillio is so very beautiful it doesn't need to have a flower to overshadow it."

"Wow! I can't wait to see what it looks like." His tummy rumbled again and reminded him that he needed to be off.

"Effel, see you later!" and he sped back to the cottage, very happy to find that breakfast was in fact ready and waiting for him, prepared by his dad as head chef and sous chef, Biffy.

After breakfast because it was raining Biffy asked Peter to teach him how to play chess and they spent a couple of hours trying to get the rules of the game fixed into Biffy's head. When he concentrated he really wasn't too bad as an opponent.

"You've done well, Biffy, for a beginner!"

Biffy looked quite pleased with himself. "Didn't think I would ever have the brains for that game," he announced.

"Come on Biffy, you're not a duffer. Why on earth do you think you are?"

"My dad says I'm as thick as two short planks."

"Well he's wrong. If you try hard enough you can do whatever you want! Don't you believe him."

"Thanks Dragon boy."

"Why does he hit you and your mum?"

"It's the drink that does it. He thinks he can handle it but it just makes him angry and then he lashes out. He only needs a couple and we know as soon as his cheeks go red that there's going to be a problem. He's not quite so bad when he's sober."

"Can't your mum do anything about it?"

"No, if she tries to say anything he just gets into a rage, with or without drink. He hates his job and I think sometimes he feels the same about us as well. The only one he leaves alone is Rhonda and I just hope that lasts." Rhonda was Biffy's sister and she was in the same class as Peter's sister, Alice.

Now he was talking about it Biffy couldn't seem to stop himself. "He always says that we held him back from making something of himself. He can't change his job because he has to provide for us all – that's what he thinks anyway! He discounts what my poor mum earns. She works herself to the bone cleaning two different offices which means she has to be out of the house by five in the morning so she's finished before the staff arrive. Then she has another job in a supermarket during the day and after all of that there is still the house to keep tidy, and the cooking, and then she has to wait on him hand and foot! It's just not fair at all! He takes every penny she earns and just hands out enough for housekeeping and clothes for us all. He drinks the rest away. I know that because once mum let slip about it after he'd hit her one time. She said I should feel sorry for him as he's just very unhappy, but why should he make everyone else's life horrid just because he is?!"

Peter was at a loss for words, he kept thinking how awful it had been for him when Biffy had been bullying him – it was almost like copying what his dad did. For all that, he couldn't imagine what it was like living in a house where you never knew when you were going to be beaten or what was going to happen. It sounded an awful life.

"Peter?" Biffy asked hesitantly.

"Yes."

"You won't tell anyone at school about this, will you? I never let anyone else know what life is like at home."

"No, I'll keep shtum, I promise. I might tell my dad though if he says anything, if that's OK with you?"

"Yeah! I like your dad. He's cool!"

"I think so too! Shall we go out for a while now the rain has dried up?"

Wearing their coats and wellies they ventured out into the fresh air. It smelt lovely – of wet loam and sea air mixed with a bit of peat and they scrabbled about on the rocks the other side of the beach from where McDragon usually rested. Effel was nowhere in sight so Peter guessed she'd gone hunting for some food.

CHAPTER NINETEEN

It was amazing how quickly time passed as they enjoyed themselves and as the weather was so good Biffy offered to go to see if he could help make their lunch so they could eat it on the beach. He was gone for quite a long time obviously enjoying the task he had set himself and Peter was content having a little space and time for himself. There was still no sign of Effel although he thought he could see a large shape wibbling and wobbling low across the water in the distance.

Just as Biffy appeared at the door of the cottage carrying two mugs of tea and a plate of sandwiches, Peter got a tickle at the back of his neck. He'd stupidly forgotten Effel's warning to him and he started to run back towards the house as fast as he could to get under cover.

Looking over his shoulder he spotted the small tornado spinning and whirling its way towards him scattering pebbles and sand and water everywhere as it did. He ran faster and at the same time heard Biffy yelling a warning to him. The whirlwind was closing in on him at high speed and he was panting and puffing trying so hard to put some distance between him and it. Then to his horror he saw it was accompanied by two squawkins. They were screeching loudly and it hurt his ears.

He was not too far from Biffy, when the spinning wind rushed around him and pulled him into its centre. He couldn't move! He felt like a statue! Biffy threw himself at it trying hard to reach into the swirling centre but a squawkin just batted him out of the way and he landed in a big heap by some patchy grass, the plate of sandwiches flying through the air.

The wind began to move back the way it had come and all Peter could do was watch, unable to move as Biffy leapt up, blood pouring down his face, and started to try and pound after them, a look of total horror on his face. The squawkins matched the pace of the whirlwind as it moved off back the way it had come.

As they started to speed across the sea, he could see the huge body of Effel motoring towards them. It was obviously a big effort for her, but for all that, she gave chase for quite a while until the whirlwind just outran her and there was no option but for her to turn back towards home. The squawkins had totally ignored the dragon obviously deeming her not worthy of their attention.

Peter's last view of her was her ungraceful landing near McDragon's rocks and Biffy heading towards her as fast as his legs could carry him.

* * *

As the wind twisted round and round in his enchanted prison Peter realised that he wasn't spinning with it, he was just held in an upright position in the centre. It was a very, very, strange feeling. He could see out through the rushing air and could only watch as the Isle of Harris slowly became a dot on the horizon. There were waves being thrown up beneath his feet but he wasn't getting wet, so he must be protected in some way. He felt sick to the stomach that he had been lax enough to put himself in a position where he could be taken. What a fool! How on earth was Biffy going to explain what had happened to him to his dad? Would he ever see his family again?

He felt they were rushing along, much faster than the speed boat had been able to go and they seemed to be on course for the distant bird stacks that they had passed during the boat trip to McMuran's island. It was pretty clear now who was behind everything that had been taking place and who was probably at the bottom of the missing dragons.

The wind whizzed about and finally they reached the far side of McMuran's island and shot into the back of the cave where the boat's captain had taken them into on their last visit. As it reached the opening where the two guard gargoyles that Peter and Biffy had seen before had been, Peter felt the swirling wind dissipate and he was flung forward to land in a very ungainly fashion on the rocky ground. A pair of black leather shoes, each bearing a bright shiny buckle were at his eye level. Above the shoes, both calves had thick cream long woollen socks which stopped just below the knees. Forcing his head back so he could look higher was the face of the wizard McMuran grinning evilly down at him. The magician looked very pale and wan and had sweat running down his face as he waved his wand and it flashed out at Peter. Just before he passed out, he heard McMuran mutter, "Lucky it didn't take any longer! I couldn't have controlled that wind much more!"

* * *

When he came to the wizard was nowhere in sight. He struggled to his feet groggily. The cave was lit eerily by small round balls of light which seemed to float unsuspended near the rocky roof. He looked around and could see a very small cage and a pair of eyes peering out of it. He staggered across to investigate further. He stared into the dark interior.

"Popple! Popple you're here!"

She looked quite forlorn. She lifted her head to look hopelessly at him.

The tiny dragon was imprisoned inside the small cube. Peter stretched his arm out tentatively towards the bars of the cage and that tickle which announced magic immediately flared up at the back of his neck. He closed his fingers around one of the bars and was thrown backwards, landing awkwardly onto the cool ground. The cage itself was made up entirely of swannee rope, which had been magicked to form the tiny prison. He stood up and shook himself down and then risked getting another shock as he tried to pull at the swannee rope prison, trying to move it. All that happened was that he was repelled, yet again, and bounced off the hard floor thumping his head hard. It hurt!

This was a nightmare surely! From his uncomfortable position, Peter pinched himself. Not a dream then!

He heard footsteps sounding like they were coming down steps and McMuran's kilt appeared, swaying about his skinny hairy legs. The sporran was hanging round his waist, just like it had been when Peter had first met him. Peter had only ever been that close to the wizard once, and that was when he first met him and shook his hand. His neck started tickling its magical warning.

He staggered to his feet, his head was banging.

"Good! You're awake laddie and you've been testing out my little prison I see!" he laughed. "It's impenetrable!"

"What have you done to the dragon that's inside?" He felt he shouldn't call Popple by her name, just in case it might give McMuran more power over her.

"What's her name boyo?"

"Dragon?" he shrugged his shoulders trying to look as if he didn't know.

"You must know! You're in league with those dragons! Tell me what it is!"

"How would I know? I can't speak to them!" he lied.

"I don't believe you!" McMuran shouted and he flipped his wand out of his sporran making his kilt swing from side to side.

Peter glared back at him. No way was he going to give in, no matter what happened to him.

A flash of stars came out of the end of the wand and Peter was dropped to the ground again. Again, he was out for the count.

CHAPTER TWENTY

When Peter came to he found he was tied down on a rock close to Popple's cage, strips of swannee securing him tightly in place. He pulled and tugged but he couldn't free himself. The tiny young dragon looked out at him sadly as if to say that it was no use. This must be rather like the etching in the dragon seers' cave that Effel had seen.

He found he could move his head about relatively easily and checked to ensure they were on their own.

"Are you OK?" he whispered to her. "Blink your eyes once for "yes" and twice for "no"."

Her eyelids fluttered down over her amethyst eyes – once.

"Good! Now we need to think of a way to get free. This swannee rope is incredibly tough! There's no give in it at all!" He tried to wriggle about but he was very tightly strapped down and he eventually had to sink back down against the stone, his breath panting because of the effort he had been making. His resting place was very uncomfortable.

Once he'd got his breath back Peter fought and fought

with the swannee rope but it just wouldn't shift at all. Popple stared out at him, there was not a lot of room for her to move about in the little cage which was the size of a small orange box. Peter thought it was a shame she was not old enough to breathe fire because then she might have been able to burn a hole in her prison.

Footsteps echoed throughout the cavern announcing the arrival of McMuran. Once he reached Peter he thrust a straw into the boy's mouth.

"Drink this!"

Peter considered refusing then realised he needed strength from wherever he could get it, and he was hungry. It tasted disgusting.

The man then held out another bottle and poked a straw through the swannee bars. Popple obediently sucked on it. Peter realised that she must have done that before. He wondered what was in her drink and, more's to the point, what was in his! At least the wizard was keen to keep them alive – for now.

"Now boyo, what is the dragon's name? I know you know it!"

"I told you… I DON'T KNOW IT! What do you want it for anyway?"

"I need to know her name so that she will become mine. My own dragon at long last! Just as she was meant to be when she hatched, except you stole her egg from me!"

It seemed the magician was getting angry yet again. He seemed to have quite a temper on him.

"Why did you bring me here anyway?" Which was a brave question considering the mood of the chap.

"So you could tell me her name of course!"

"Well, the other dragon didn't do your bidding and you seemed to know his name." Peter was referring to Spit.

"Hrmmph!" Peter could see and hear McMuran's feet pacing around the cave, backwards and forwards. Maybe that thought hadn't crossed his mind before. Why hadn't Spit bonded with the wizard? It was a mystery even to Peter himself and he decided he'd ponder on this when they were on their own again. He rather thought McMuran would keep him alive so long as he thought Peter might have the answer for him.

He heard a slithering kind of noise at the back of the cave and tried to turn his head to see what it was. With great difficulty, he squinted into the darkness and then his skin crawled when he realised it was that nasty Slider, McMuran's second in command. McMuran went over to him and they whispered together and left the cave.

Peter relaxed again.

"Are you still OK?" he muttered through a closed mouth.

Popple blinked once.

"Good! Don't worry, I'm positive that Seraphina and Haribald will find a way to rescue us somehow." He wasn't really that sure but if he could do nothing else at least he could try and keep Popple's spirits up – she was only a baby after all.

"Just remember, if McMuran does try and bond you with him you must be strong in your mind, and resist. OK?"

She blinked once again.

He puffed out a big sigh as he considered their situation. It did seem that they were trapped until they

113

could find how to burst through the swannee rope. There must be a way!

Maybe, just maybe, they would let him go when he needed the loo…but then of course how could he go anywhere when it would mean leaving Popple behind him and he could hardly swim away from the island. He would freeze and drown if he did and she couldn't fly.

Gradually his eyelids closed and he nodded off to sleep. It wasn't at all dreamless, more of a nightmare about dragons and squawkins and… McMuran! He woke up, thrashing about as much as the rope would let him, and realised he was shouting very loudly. Oh no! He was calling Popple's name!

Feet rushed into the cavern.

"Ha, now I have her name!" The kilt bounced up and down as the wizard became so energised and excited. "She will be mine!" Then he turned to sneer at Peter, "You shouldn't be so trusting about taking drink from an enemy, it contained a sleeping potion. It had the exact effect I hoped it would!" Boasting.

"Did you drug the dragon's drink as well?"

"No, I wouldn't want anything to muddle her mind. It needs to be clear when she bonds with me."

Slider shuffled into vision, hovering at the back of the cavern holding a length of swannee rope. McMuran nodded at him and flicked his wand at the cage. A small door opened up and the nasty slimy person came forward to reach into the cage and wrap the rope around poor Popple's neck. Popple was dragged out into the open, fighting every inch of the way. After all she was a dragon, no matter how small, and was quite strong. She snapped angrily at Slider trying to bite his arm. He just pulled harder and McMuran added his strength to the effort until they finally manoeuvred her to the other side of the cavern.

McMuran began to wave his wand about in front of her tiny face and a glowing figure of eight appeared just by her nose. He started to intone, using her name at the beginning of every sentence.

"Popple! Popple! Resist. Fight it! Don't look at him!" screamed Peter. "Look at me instead! Me! Me! Me!" She was twisting and turning as the swannee rope got tighter and tighter. McMuran spun round…!

Bang!

Peter's head slammed down onto the rock beneath him. Then, blackness!

CHAPTER TWENTY ONE

It was totally silent in the cave when Peter's eyes flickered open. Ouch! His head hurt. He felt a drum was banging inside of his brain, so he closed his eyes again.

Staring through half closed eyelids he looked across to where McMuran had been trying to magic Popple into bonding with him. There was no-one in sight.

He moaned.

"Popple, where are you!" A slight scratching noise could be heard over to his right and groaning he twisted his head to look in that direction. Thank goodness, there she was inside her prison again.

"Did…did… he make you bond with him?" he stuttered through dry lips.

She blinked twice and he felt himself relax down into the rock.

"Are you OK?"

One blink.

"Oh, thank goodness for that! We need to think of a plan, and quickly, because we're now back where we started. Trapped on an island in the middle of nowhere."

Random thoughts whizzed around his head as he tried to clear the massive headache he had.

"I don't suppose you know where McDragon is do you?"

One blink of the eye.

"Is he here somewhere?"

Another blink.

She looked over towards the back of the cavern and then back at Peter.

"Is there another cave at the back of this one?"

One blink.

That was something good he supposed. If by chance they could break out then maybe the big dragon could escape too and carry them away from the island. At that thought, the headache seemed to ease a little.

"I'm sorry it came to this Popple but keep your hopes up, we'll find a way to escape, I'm sure!"

A voice inside Peter's head whispered, "Wishful thinking!"

There was silence for a while. Peter could hear the sea slurping into the cave and then out again. It was quite soothing somehow. The cave smelt damp and minerally. He thought he heard something creeping about somewhere near the cave entrance and when he looked in that direction he imagined he saw a pale face. At that very moment McMuran came down the stone steps behind them and Peter focussed on him instead. The wizard looked as if he was in a massive rage as he approached them.

"I don't know what you did boy! You must have done something! It didn't work!"

"Good!" Peter was thinking deeply, it was strange that the name had not worked and then he had a light bulb moment!

"I can see you know why! Tell me NOW!"

"No way!" Peter shouted back at him.

McMuran's face was beginning to turn beetroot red. He was obviously in a huge temper and he flicked his wand around the cave. Sparks bounced off of the walls, faster and faster, going this way and that, totally out of control. Then with a loud bang... which under different circumstances would have made Peter laugh, there was a big flash and the smell of burning as McMuran's hair was set alight.

With a loud yell of pain, he turned and ran up the stairs behind him.

"Serves him right!"

"I agree," said a voice at the cave entrance. "So that's a wizard! You do seem to have got yourself into a bit of bother Dragon boy!"

Peter's face was quite a picture. "Biffy! How on earth did you get here?"

"Time for questions later Petersmith. He'll be back and this could be the only chance we have!"

Biffy slipped his hand into his coat sleeve and pulled out a flat green stick which was almost the same length as the distance from his elbow to his wrist. It tapered down to a small pink stubby ending.

"Don't move whatever you do! This is incredibly sharp!"

Brandishing the stick in the air Biffy moved closer to the rock. There was a slicing noise, and Peter felt the swannee rope round his legs burst apart. Then the next line of rope, followed by the last one and finally he was free. He could sit up.

"Help Popple please! We must get her out. He wants to get her to bond with him."

"Hi Popple. Pleased to meet you!" Biffy smiled at the little dragon as he approached her cage. "Move back, little one," and he reached forward and sliced diagonally across the front of the swannee bars, then wiggled his stick from side to side making a doorway for her to slip through. Peter noticed as he did that the tiny pink end on the stick got darker and darker until it was glowing red. Although he desperately wanted to have answers to his questions he quite agreed that this wasn't the time to talk.

Biffy smiled at Peter, "See I knew I had the right name for you, Dragon boy!" Peter grinned back.

As soon as Popple was free she staggered about a bit. The cage hadn't allowed her any room to move about so she was rather stiff.

"Can she go out the way you came in Biffy?"

"Yes, but…" he looked at the little dragon, "Can you swim Popple? I can't see any other way to escape."

"Can you Popple?"

A blink.

"That means yes. Show her the way please Biffy, and quickly! But wait! What about the gargoyle guards at the entrance? They are really evil squawkins and they will hurt her."

"They're not there. They're hunting for Effel at the moment," was the matter of fact answer.

"Oh! Right, urm well," Peter was rather shocked at

Biffy's casual comment, "I'll have to catch you up. Popple believes McDragon is over in that direction." Peter waved his hand towards the back of the cave.

"Dragon boy! You'll need me if McDragon is tied up as you were!"

"Can't I have your sharp stick?"

"No Peter! It will cut you to shreds. It doesn't affect me. Can you come with us and we'll find Popple a place to hide safely and then we can search together? We might not find one another otherwise."

"But Popple should be our main concern as McMuran wants to enslave her. I have to go Biffy and find McDragon. I just have this gut feeling that there is no choice. Please?"

The other boy nodded slowly.

"Come Popple! Follow me! Peter, I'll return in a jiffy once I have Popple in the water. But be careful. The magician could be back at any moment!" As he ran out of the cavern with Popple scuttling after him, Peter could hear Biffy sensibly giving Popple instructions about how to duck down in the water if she heard anything. He seemed to be taking the whole situation totally in his stride. He also told her help was on its way.

The little dragon stopped at the cavern entrance and looked back at Peter over her shoulder, obviously not at all happy about leaving him behind.

"Go Popple! Please go! I will be with you soon!"

Peter was nearly at the back of the cavern when he heard footsteps echoing down the stone staircase that McMuran used.

"Go quickly! I can hear him coming!"

He listened carefully as he crept across towards the

back of the cave moving towards the right past the steps and started to make his way down a long but very wide tunnel which was lit by yet more small round balls of light which bounced up and down near the ceiling. He knew he had to move as quietly as possible but at the same time it was quite a long straight distance to where he could see the end and there wasn't anywhere to hide if he needed to. The walls were very smooth.

He heard running and shouting but his dragon senses told him that the magician wasn't following him – he must have gone to where the sea met the cave. He really hoped that Popple had done as Biffy instructed and had submerged herself under the water managing to stay hidden below the surface.

There was quite a strong stench of something very familiar drifting along the tunnel. Very familiar. McDragon! He tiptoed as fast as he could, trying to ensure that he didn't scuffle any loose pebbles which would let McMuran know where he was.

A sound behind him made him leap to the side of the tunnel and press himself against the smooth rock hoping, rather feebly, that there was enough shadow to hide him.

"Psst! It's me!"

Peter waited and very quietly for a big boy, Biffy came up beside him.

"How did you get past McMuran?"

"He was too busy searching for Popple." Seeing Peter's look of horror, he touched him gently on the arm, "It's OK Dragon boy, she swims well and was nearly out of the cavern when I last saw her. I told her to keep submerged if she could and once she was out in the sea she should turn into the rocks at the side and find somewhere where she could clamber onto a rock and wait for rescue. She's rather cute, isn't she?"

"Yeah, I love her to bits!"

"Wait, Dragon boy! I have to do something."

Biffy routed around in his pocket and pulled out a big dragon scale. It had a turquoise tint to it.

"How did you get that? That's mine!"

"I'll tell you later."

Biffy went very quiet – he was obviously communicating via the scale.

"Let's move on. I've told Seraphina where she should find her tiny dragonling."

Peter looked even more shocked, as he silently and carefully carried on his journey towards the larger light at the end of the tunnel. Biffy seemed to know everything about the dragons!

The smell was getting worse and it was very hard not to choke and cough, but finally they arrived in an open cavern. A lot of the space in the cave was taken up by a great big black dragon with gold sprinkles along the top of him. He wasn't in a cage but secured by long swannee ropes around his neck which were affixed to clamps in the walls either side of him. There were also restraints around his four huge legs which were also attached to the walls in the same way.

"McDragon!" Peter whispered.

"Petersmith! I knew you would come, but it is not safe for you!"

Biffy stepped into the cave close behind Peter.

"McDragon," he said, bowing his head in deference to the dragon, "I am pleased to meet with you."

McDragon nodded his head back to the boy.

"Young Biffy!" he acknowledged the bigger lad.

Looking about him Peter could see a huge pile of dragon excrement over to one side and this was what was obviously making such an awful smell. He wrinkled up his nose.

"Peter! Peter! I can hear McMuran coming down the tunnel. We must hide!"

"Go up through the entrance over there," McDragon indicated with his nose somewhere behind the pile of poo.

"We'll be back, McDragon! I promise!"

The boys ran, skirting round the mess very carefully. They didn't want any of that on their feet! McDragon was right, there was a tunnel entrance, which was lit as the other one had been by the round lights. Not far along it were steps leading upwards and they climbed them, Peter easily, but Biffy was panting.

"Try to be quiet Biffy, or McMuran will hear you!"

"I'm…." puff puff, "doing my best Dragon boy!"

At the top of the steps Peter pushed through some overhanging ivy and walked out into a familiar sight – he was in the enchanted dome where he and Spit had found, and rescued, the dragon Pearl. In fact, he was amazed to find they had emerged inside the huge cathedral of the dragon skeleton of Arletta, which was where Spit and Peter had hidden to watch Slider entering into the small building where the Pearl was being incubated. The building was now just a ruin. The wizard's fire must have done that.

"This way, Biffy! Over here!"

They crunched out of the skeleton and into some bushes behind what was left of the old building. Peter threw himself down on the ground, peering out carefully through the big leaves. Biffy did the same, trying desperately to catch his breath. And they waited.

And waited.

Eventually a furious McMuran appeared inside the rib bones of the skeleton, Slider just behind him.

"Where have they gone to? I bet that boy has led the little dragon to where he got in and out of the dome before. There's no way he can release the black dragon from his tethers. Come on, we'll soon catch him! You can kill the boy but keep the dragon alive at all costs!"

Peter gulped at that as they watched the nasty evil pair continue on their way in the opposite direction to where Peter and Biffy were hiding.

Peter put his hand onto the other boy indicating they should wait a few moments just in case McMuran or Slider doubled back. It was very difficult not to just dash off back to McDragon, but wait they did.

CHAPTER TWENTY TWO

At long last Peter deemed that it was safe enough for them to move, and they crept out of their hiding place back over to the age-old dragon bones. Peter wondered how he had missed the entrance to the caves the last time he'd been there, but had to admit it merged nicely into the wall beside it and was almost impossible to see unless you knew where it was. They leapt down the steep steps and almost flew into the cavern where the enormous dragon was imprisoned.

"Petersmith! How did you get past the wizard?"

"We hid in the bushes near where Arletta's bones are."

McDragon looked sad. "Ah, yes! Poor Arletta. It was because of her bones that I ended up here. Maybe she was captured the same way."

While they were talking, Biffy brandished his cutting tool. The tip had turned back to a gentle pink colour but as he sliced easily through the bonds that trapped McDragon it began to turn red as it had before.

McDragon looked at the stick, "Amazing, you have the stalk of a frillio and it doesn't cut you"

Biffy carried on with his task, "Effel thought I should bring this with me, just in case. It's lucky the frillio decided to produce a spike just at the right time! There, you're free!" Biffy talked about Effel so matter of factly, as if it was normal for a boy to speak to a dragon.

McDragon shook his big body and lifted one foot at a time off of the cavern floor.

"Everything seems to be working properly so let's leave this place quickly!"

"Do you think you can get through this tunnel McDragon?" called Peter as he headed towards the big tunnel entrance.

"Ah, yes, that is the way they brought me in."

As they moved through the tunnel McDragon explained how he'd got there.

"That man has very strong powers... very strong indeed! A whirlwind blew over my resting place and circled round me and as it did I felt this strong compulsion to visit Arletta's skeleton, even though my instinct told me it was a bad thing to do. Looking back, McMuran must have put some magic into the whirlwind which altered my thinking because although I was fighting every inch of the way here, I still flew to the island under my own steam. I walked as if in a daze down this tunnel and was captured in the same spot as where you found me. The only good bit was when I noticed how exhausted the wizard was after working his magic on me. He's truly evil!"

They finally came to a halt at the end of the long tunnel and Biffy slipped out to check there wasn't a surprise party waiting for them in the next cave.

It was empty.

Just before McDragon stepped into the cold sea he breathed heat onto both boys and then manoeuvred his huge body down into the water, at the same time making sure his long barbed tail did not sweep either of them into the water.

"I'm not at all sure Biffy, that I have warmed you up but it will put heat into your clothes. Hold on tightly to Peter and hopefully some of his heat will transfer over to you." Biffy nodded to let McDragon know he understood.

"Now climb aboard and I will swim out of the cave. Talon's crossed there are no squawkins on the hunt for us outside!"

The sea covered their feet and legs, and it was very, very, cold but the rest of them was dry.

Biffy pressed himself closely against Peter's back as instructed. The sound of the water's ebb and flow echoed around the beautiful cave. It made a lovely shushing sound. Peter checked either side of the fissure in the rock they had just emerged from, but fortunately there were no gargoyle guards watching them. Dragon scales locked down on their knees to keep them safely in place.

McDragon used his powerful tail to move them towards the entrance but just as they reached the opening, a huge shadow seemed to engulf them and a big body swooped down close to them. McDragon seemed unperturbed but both boys were almost shaking with fear.

"Seraphina! Do you have Popple?"

"I'm looking for her now. I think she is on a rock close by. By the by, it's good to see you at last McDragon. I'll return to my island once I have Popple. Poor Spit is by himself and is nearly out of his mind with worry about

Popple, you, and his friend, Petersmith. Well done Master Biffy!" She swept past them.

McDragon swam strongly forward. Peter felt nice and warm and not at all wet but he was sure he could hear Biffy's teeth chattering.

"Biffy, where did you say Effel was?" he asked.

"She was leading the squawkins a merry dance."

"I'm not sure she's a good enough flier to dodge them."

"Well I don't know what to compare her to as far as a dragon flying is concerned but it was rather like being on a roller coaster ride… very up and down and then slow and then fast."

"Maybe that'll be in her favour then. They won't be used to that."

At that moment, they watched Seraphina swoop down and snatch up a small shape over by the rocks a little way from the cavern's entrance. Then, with a loud roar, she was up, up and away, flying over the top of them and off into the distance.

"Ready yourselves boys! Hold on very tight!" boomed McDragon's voice. "I think I can manage the two of you… just!"

Biffy's arms tightened around Peter's waist as McDragon's huge wings spread out across the top of the water. They glided up and down splashing water everywhere and then with a final big effort the dragon raised himself out of the black sea. Higher and higher until the island was behind them.

"What's that on the island?" asked Biffy. "That big bubble?"

"You can see it? That's the magic dome that we were in when we saw the dragon skeleton."

"Wow!" breathed Biffy in his ear. "Oh, there is the wizard! He's just outside the bubble! I bet the wind is making him cold in that kilt!" and he chuckled. Peter joined in as he looked down and saw McMuran waving his arms about, his kilt flapping up and down. He released a huge blast of fire from his wand which gathered wind up and it began to spin and whiz its way towards them.

"Look out McDragon!"

The dragon dived downwards, his neck and head in line with his body and his tail straight out behind him. There were golden and red flames enclosed inside the whirlwind which rushed past them but then it turned to come at them again.

McDragon pulled himself out of the dive and started to rise up. The whirlwind followed, it was so very close, it could swallow them up. As it got very near to them Biffy stretched out his arm wielding the frillio stick and holding it out as far as it would go. He prodded at the whirlwind and the top third of it sliced off and broke away. He slashed at it again and another part suffered the same fate. On its own the last part of it was far too feeble and all Biffy had to do was to prod it to make it burst open and pop, much like a balloon would and then it too dispersed.

"Amazing! That frillio knife is fantastic!" shouted Peter.

"Too right!" Biffy yelled back.

They both thought they could hear a loud howl of anger coming across the air to them. "I guess that must be that wizard! He sounds very upset!"

"Serves him right!" Peter replied.

"Petersmith!" McDragon's voice echoed in their heads, "Please can you look out for squawkins! We do not want to be taken unawares as I am not sure how I will manage with two of you riding on me."

Almost as he had finished speaking there was that awful screeching sound coming from somewhere above them.

"There are three of them above us McDragon! Look out!"

With his tail pointing straight behind him and his head and neck in line with his body, McDragon went into another dive. At the very last moment when it seemed that he would submerge himself under the water he managed to get himself horizontal and fly across the top of the waves. The squawkins continued coming down towards them and Biffy, yet again, sat poised as he reached out with the frillio knife, ready to strike.

As the lead squawkin made its first attack, Biffy stabbed it in the eye. It screamed even louder than before and splashed howling into the sea. Then there was a horrifying roar above them and seemingly out of nowhere a huge spout of dragon's fire scorched the second squawkin. It too tumbled into the deep sea.

"What ho Haribald! Good timing!"

If Haribald had been a soldier he would have saluted to Peter as he sped onwards and upwards towards the final squawkin. He was a very angry and fierce dragon. They should not have taken his little Popple.

Once he had despatched the last squawkin down to the wet depths Haribald returned and flew in tandem with McDragon.

Peter could feel Biffy was shivering quite badly and he asked Haribald if there was any way he could warm his friend up.

"I can try Petersmith. Biffy, be ready for some heat. It will be like fire blowing around you as the heat that McDragon uses on Peter obviously doesn't work on you." There was a puff and then fire seemed to envelop both boys, so that Peter felt his cheeks get quite red.

"Th...thank you! That feels so much better!" stuttered Biffy and gradually Peter could feel the shivering stopped.

There was silence for a while apart from the sound of the wind whooshing past the two pairs of huge wings. Then another strange wheezing sound came from behind them. It seemed to be getting louder and louder and closer, rather like bellows being pumped up and down. Peter checked behind them and there was poor Effel puffing and panting as she struggled to catch them up, bits of fire blew in and out of her nostrils in time with her breathing. Peter could see the rents in her wings which seemed to be far worse than before.

At long last Effel reached McDragon's other side and the lovely sound of dragon humming vibrated around them all. As usual Effel's sound was somewhat out of tune but it was still good to hear. Peter smiled with delight, and he heard Biffy whisper to him, "That's amazing Dragon boy!"

"Yeah! I agree totally!"

He could feel Biffy rootling around in his pocket and then he said, "Dragon boy?"

"Yes Biffy?"

"I am feeling some strange thoughts. Something is asking what is happening?"

"I guess that is Spit. Please can you say this out loud, "Seraphina is on her way home to you with Popple. Everyone is fine.""

"Okey dokey," then Biffy relayed the message to Spit.

"He said, "Over and Out! See you soon Petersmith!""

With a grin, Peter answered, "That's my friend Spit!"

"I would like to meet him."

"You will Biffy. I am sure you will."

"Oh no!"

"What's up?"

"Your dad let me make a cake and I left it in the oven when I came out to bring our lunch! It'll be black by now, that's if it hasn't set fire to the oven!"

"Don't worry! We'll be in dragon time – you'll see, the cake will be fine!"

CHAPTER TWENTY THREE

The boys were soon back on dry land, safe and sound. Once they'd dismounted the three dragons arrayed themselves in front of the boys. The dragon song echoed around them again and Peter joined in as he usually did. Biffy rather hesitantly joined in, his hum gradually getting stronger and louder.

When the tune had finished Haribald spoke, "Thank you so much you laddies for saving my Popple!"

McDragon made it clear that he too was delighted with their efforts in rescuing him.

"I knew you would succeed, Petersmith! You are most definitely dragon kin."

"But without Biffy, we wouldn't have managed." Peter told him.

Biffy interjected, "It was a team effort I think! If the magician hadn't taken Peter then Effel might not have shown herself to me, so I think we all deserve a pat on the back! It was amazing!" He wrinkled up his nose, "What's that smell? It's rather like something has gone rotten! Urgh! It seems to be coming from me!"

As he said it he pulled out the frillio stick. "Oh no! It's died!" The stick had gone all soggy and the tiny flower on the tip was yellow and that was where the smell was coming from. It was rather like rotting compost.

"They only have a very short life Biffy, but no matter there will be another one sometime!" said Effel encouragingly. "Throw it in the sea because the smell will only get worse."

Biffy lobbed it into the water and they watched the retreating tide gradually draw it out to sea.

The plan was that McDragon and Effel would take the lads to Seraphina's hideaway the next day. Effel felt it was a matter of pride that she carried the larger boy after their rescue yesterday and assured them she would be quite strong enough so long as she had a rest and a good feed. Biffy looked a little dubious but there was no way he was going to offend a dragon. Haribald made his goodbyes and leapt elegantly into the air to start his journey home.

It was quite a relief to trudge back towards the cottage where, to Biffy's absolute delight and amazement, his cake was not quite ready.

"See! I told you it would be alright because of dragon time!"

"Wow! You need to tell me all about that and everything else. It's all so amazing!"

"Didn't dad say he was going to take us somewhere today?"

"Yes… Do you mean we have to go out again?"

"Oh yes, otherwise it would look very odd. Where are we going?"

"I think he said he needed to drive to Stornaway to get something for his laptop. But isn't that miles away?"

"Yup! About fifty miles, but dad did mention something about fish and chips while we are there."

"Good, because I'm starving!"

Once the cake had cooled they both had huge slices of it to tide them over. They'd missed the lunch that Biffy had made because it was discarded somewhere on the beach when Peter was taken, but the cake was really delicious.

"You can make us that again Biffy, you seem to have the touch."

The other boy looked embarrassed, "Well, I seem to rather like cooking. Your dad says I can help him do dinner tomorrow and I'm really looking forward to that!"

* * *

They had a great time in Stornoway eating their fish and chips on the harbour wall and watching the gulls fighting over titbits, and the seals which were bobbing up and down. They both nodded off in the car going back to the cottage much to Peter's dad's amusement.

"You must have eaten too much if it wore you out so you both had to have a nap!" his dad joked when eventually they started their walk back to the cottage along the cliff top.

* * *

The lads went up to Peter's bedroom as soon as they got home. Finally, it was time to find out what had happened to each of them. At least Peter was released from his promise not to tell anyone about the dragons, as Biffy had now met them, which meant he could talk freely.

He was a bit upset to find his room had been turned over and Biffy apologised and said he would explain why soon. They spent a little time putting everything away until it was just how Peter liked it and then they sat on the bed sharing a big chocolate bar that Peter's dad had given them.

"You start Peter, tell me how you met the dragons in the first place."

Rather hesitantly at first, Peter related all that had happened to him the first time he'd been in Harris. How he discovered that McDragon had been waiting for him to arrive because it had been written in the seers' cave that Petersmith would find the missing Pearl. Then about Spit, who Biffy was so looking forward to meeting. He'd already seen Archie that day on the beach when he spotted Peter talking to him. Peter looked so proud when he explained he'd been asked to name Popple after she'd hatched from her Pearl.

"That's the answer to why McMuran couldn't bond with her when he used her name!" Peter exclaimed.

"Why?"

"Well, her nickname is Popple, but her full name is Popsicle!"

"Cool name!" responded Biffy.

"Yeah, I thought it suited her as she was popping about even though she was tiny."

Then it was Biffy's turn to tell his story.

"Well, I put my cake in the oven and as I told you I

came to bring you our lunch. As I started down the beach I saw the whirlwind take you accompanied by those two, what did you call them?"

"Squawkins."

"Well they have a really gut wrenching screech don't they?"

"They do indeed. McDragon says that's why they are called squawkins. They have evolved from the original gargoyles that were magicked to life by a wizard when he had a fight with another wizard. What's more if the poison on the end of their talons touches us we could die."

Biffy shivered at that thought.

"I ran as fast as I could but got there just as they were taking off with you and thrust my arm in to try and pull you out. I was thrown to the ground. Couldn't do anything about it! As they lifted off, I was totally shocked when a huge dragon came chasing after you. Eventually it returned after the whirlwind got away and it crashed down onto the beach, bottoming out and careered off as it slid along the shingle. She landed in a big heap having come up against the rocks. That Effel, she's not too good at landing, is she?"

"She hasn't had much practice for years and years. You know I first met her when we were at camp."

"So that's why you kept disappearing! I wondered what was going on when I saw you on the back of something flying off into the distance. Thought I was hallucinating!"

"That was the first time she'd flown for such a long time and I actually thought we were going to end up in the loch, she was so bad at keeping aloft."

"Don't think she's improved that much even now," laughed Biffy, "when I saw the other dragons flying and then heard her puffing and blowing fire alongside them I wanted to laugh. She's very holey isn't she and rather battered?"

"That's because she is ancient," answered Peter. "She's a dragon seer now and doesn't do much flying. One day perhaps we can go to the dragon seers' cave so you can see the amazing predictions the dragon seers have made. It'd be interesting to see what they have to show about you. They had sketched me saving Popple's Pearl and that is why the dragons thought I would be the one to save them."

"Really! Oh… I'd love to see that!"

"So, what happened to you next Biffy?"

"It was a shock enough for me seeing a dragon but then she spoke to me! How amazing is that?! Her first words in my head were, 'Close your mouth boy, I expect you haven't seen a dragon landing before.'"

"Well you probably won't see one landing like that ever!" giggled Peter.

"It was very messy! There were stones and sand spraying everywhere. Anyhow, I was so shocked I couldn't speak for a while and eventually she dragged herself upright and turned to face me. She has such terrible bad breath! I think I'll clean my teeth more often in future!" That made Peter snort.

"Then she said, 'We have to find a way to save Petersmith and you are key to the plan!' I didn't hesitate but just answered, 'Yes'. I didn't even question her name for you, it just seemed um… right somehow."

"She answered, 'Good! They'll have taken him to that evil wizard McMuran and I guess that it must be on that island you visited in the boat. Petersmith mentioned that there were gargoyles guarding an entrance in the cave and that one winked at him.' You never said anything about that Dragon boy!"

"Well, I had sworn an oath to McDragon that I wouldn't tell anyone about the dragons, and anyhow… you'd never have believed me, would you?!"

"True! So Effel asked to see what I now know is the dragon scale I stole from your washbag while we were away. I always meant to put it back but it fascinated me so much. It made my neck tickle whenever I touched it. Sorry, Peter, that's another thing I've done which is totally wrong!"

"It's OK, Effel said I should let you keep it because you could get in touch with Spit for me, and you did, although you didn't realise you were doing it of course. Effel thought it wouldn't be safe for me to talk to Spit through it because it might help McMuran in some way."

"Well, she asked me to give Spit a message about your capture and for him to tell Seraphina if he saw her. Spit was very upset that she hadn't returned and neither had, what was his name, Hariboo?"

"Haribald. Actually, it's Haribald d'Ness. He usually lives in Loch Ness and, apparently, he is what humans have glimpsed on occasion and think is the Loch Ness monster. That amuses the dragons!"

"I guess it does! Anyhow what upset Spit even more was that you'd been taken and he couldn't fly well enough to help save you. He got quite cross about it.

Effel told me to look for a big dragon scale which was hidden somewhere in your room and looked much the same as the little one I had and she sent me to go and find it. That's why I left your room in a such a mess. It took me quite a while to find the scale, you'd hidden it very well and I realised there was some urgency in getting back to her."

"Not to worry, at least we've tidied it up now."

"So," Biffy stopped suddenly, "I can't quite believe all this! It's so astounding really!"

A nod from Peter and he continued.

"I took the big scale back to Effel and she told me to hold it firmly and then I had to relay a message to Seraphina about you and where she thought you'd been taken. As the dragon seers' etchings had shown a picture of you with Popple she guessed that Popple would be there as well.

She told Effel, through me as her mouthpiece, that she would meet us at the island. Then we flew there. Wow! Fancy me flying on a dragon! And when those scales snapped down on my knees I just felt so secure. I've tried riding a horse and that feels so unsafe, almost as if I'm going to fall off at any moment. A dragon is so much easier, apart from the bit where I had to climb on." That made Peter snigger because in the past McDragon had had to help him up by pushing him with his snout. Peter's bad hand made it quite hard to hang on while he climbed up the shiny scales.

"Well, you know how up and down the ride is on Effel," another nod from Peter, "my poor stomach. I kept thinking I was going to lose my breakfast all down her shoulder."

"Yeah, and there would have been carrots in it! Even though we haven't eaten any."

"Before we left though she told me to pick the flower on its stalk out of the frillio. She said it wouldn't hurt me because I am non-magical, which was news to me, and when we were flying she told me how it could slice through anything and that I would need it. Also, to make sure I didn't let you use it as it would cut your hands to pieces.

When we finally arrived at the island Seraphina was nowhere in sight so I guess her journey must have been a lot longer than ours was. Effel got me to lift my legs up on her back and then she swam into the cave and helped me out onto the rock. I have no idea how she managed without soaking me. At that point, the gargoyles came to life, emerging from the rocks and she had to manoeuvre herself out of the cave very quickly. Quite a feat for her! They were only a little way behind her because it took so long for her to get up into the air. Luckily, it took them a little while to transform into squawkins and when they did get out of the cavern I could hear them screeching and had to cover my ears. You know what happened next because I came into the cavern very quietly and as magic cannot affect me, McMuran didn't sense that I was there."

CHAPTER TWENTY FOUR

The boys chatted for quite a while. Peter felt happy that at last he had someone who he could talk to about dragons other than Spit. Also, he was hoping that Effel would tell him he could use the scale now to speak to the little dragon. He was looking forward to going to Seraphina's island the next day and, rather strangely, quite excited about showing off to his new friend. Peter warned Biffy that he would need to be up early if they were going visiting and although Biffy wasn't an early riser, he agreed that he would get up if Peter would wake him.

They both slept soundly and deeply, the trials of the day before having taken its toll of them, however next morning, as usual, Peter was up bright and early and tapping quietly on Biffy's door. He could hear the other boy groaning so Peter stuck his head round the door and just said, "Shall I go without you then?" That did the trick and it wasn't long before Biffy was beside him and they were walking down towards McDragon's rocks.

The black and gold dragon was waiting patiently for them by the edge of the sea which was lapping gently around his feet. A short distance from him stood Effel in her holey finery, looking very proud.

Peter smiled at them, it was so wonderful to see two such magnificent creatures standing together.

"What ho McDragon! What's the plan then?"

"You will ride with me Petersmith as agreed, and your friend Biffy will go with Effel."

With a sly sideways look at Biffy, Peter stepped over to McDragon and once he had been warmed by the dragon's breath he was helped on board, struggling a bit when he had to use his two-fingered and one thumbed hand. The scales locked down on his knees and he gripped hold of the upright neck scales in front of him waiting for the take off. He could see Effel was finding it tricky trying to get Biffy on board and in the end McDragon marched over to help by giving Biffy a big nudge with his long nose. The poor boy was so shocked he nearly fell down the other side of her neck. He surrounded him with hot air the same way that Haribald had done the day before in the hope it would keep him warm.

McDragon gracefully waved his big wings up and down and with a spring from his legs he took off into the blue sky, heading off towards the sun which was making fabulous patterns across the sea. Peter looked behind and he could see that Effel had had to take a long run across the beach and then launch herself across the sea. It was a big effort for her, particularly as she had a big boy on top of her so she juddered up and down with her talons hitting the top of the tiny waves as she tried to gain some height. Peter did wonder if pride was going to come before a fall, but she had been determined to carry his large friend.

After some time McDragon slowed his flight to allow Effel to catch up with them and then the two huge dragons flew side by side over the beautiful sea. Beneath them Peter spotted some porpoises leaping into the air and diving into the water, trying hard to keep up with the dragons. Peter yelled at Biffy and pointed down at them. The other boy put his thumb in the air to show he had seen them.

Peter and McDragon talked on their journey about Biffy's part in the rescue and Peter reminded McDragon about when the dragon had told him there would probably be a reason why Biffy had picked on Peter and bullied him in the past. At the time, Peter had become very angry with the dragon, but now, in hindsight, he admitted that he had been correct. Biffy's problem seemed to be his father.

On and on they flew. This time Effel didn't have to have a rest on the top of the stacks which would have been a big relief to the seabirds who lived there if they'd realised. Peter could hear her laboured breathing though, but she seemed to be managing a lot better than previously, particularly considering the trials she had been through the day before and the weight of the boy on her back.

Finally, they circled above Seraphina's tiny island and beneath them Peter saw a small dragon bouncing up and down in excitement and then Spit took off and flew up to greet them. Peter was very pleased to see that Archie was with him.

"How do you do Petersmith?!" Spit called in their traditional manner of greeting one another.

"Very well thank you Spit! How do you do?"

"Very well, thank you Petersmith!"

He stayed with them as they began to dive gracefully

down towards the flattest spot on the island. Archie thought it best to stay in the air while the dragons landed. Effel went in first and did her usual crash landing, ploughing across the top of the clearing and finally crumpling to a stop as she hit the rocks at the end. She lay there for a while and Biffy took the opportunity to scramble off as soon as her scales had released their hold on his knees.

McDragon landed quite lightly for such a big dragon and as Peter slid off he told him how much better his landing was compared to the first time they had flown together. McDragon hrumphed in response.

Spit came down beside them and as soon as his talons hit the ground he was running towards his best friend, Petersmith, and barrelled into him knocking him over. Biffy just watched in amazement. Then Popple was amongst the two of them taking pleasure in the sheer joy of their mad greeting.

Once Seraphina and Haribald ambled over to them there was the loud sound of the dragon humming song. Spit, Peter and Popple immediately stopped their bundling and joined in with the music. Peter had to smile at Effel's off key humming as she staggered across to be with them all but he realised that his tune was probably not great either. Biffy stood up straighter and then decided that he should join in as well. He looked rather embarrassed about it but his hum had a really mellow sound to it.

When the lovely happy sound had finished Peter proudly introduced Spit and Archie to Biffy. Biffy said very little because he was still quite in awe of all the dragons and astounded at the fact that Peter was so very comfortable with them.

Seraphina touched both the boys on each of their foreheads as she said, "Thank you Petersmith, you proved yet again that you are definitely dragon kin. Popple told me how you tried to keep her spirits up when you were both trapped and how you stood up to that evil magician. Thank you too, Biffy, for finding the strength to help save our Popple! We would hate to be without her and if you hadn't been so brave she wouldn't be here with us now."

Biffy's eyes welled up when he heard this, he was so very proud.

Popple too reached up, but as their foreheads were too high for her she touched each of them on their knees. Peter wrapped his arms around her small scaly neck and gave her a kiss and a cuddle. He really loved the tiny dragon.

Haribald, also touched them both on the forehead. Then all four adult dragons surrounded the two boys, who stood proudly with Spit and Popple next to them as the dragon song was hummed to the two of them. Peter felt a big warmth spread throughout his body and he knew that it must be from the song.

"Can I ask a question please?"

"Of course, Petersmith."

"Can you be sure that McMuran will not send his whirlwind or squawkins to take Popple again? What can you do to protect her?"

"We have thought long and hard on this Petersmith, and we have managed to set up magic wards around the island, much like McMuran's magic bubbledome, and this should give us all the protection we need."

"That's good to know. I would have been worrying otherwise. It would be a terrible thing if he stole her again."

Popple sidled up to Biffy and stood very close to him sniffing. The boy shyly reached out and stroked her very gently. Peter smiled at the sight and took the opportunity to move over to Spit.

"Can I use Spit's scale from now on to talk to him? Will that be safe?"

"Yes," answered Effel, "now that the wards are in place, and bearing in mind that McMuran already knows where we are, I believe that shouldn't be a problem."

Biffy reached reluctantly into his pocket and handed the small grey scale over to Peter who took it, murmuring his thanks. "It's OK Biffy, if Spit doesn't mind I can share it with you if you like." The other boy beamed his thanks. Spit nodded his agreement.

The big dragons went to the overhang of the rocks and were obviously discussing something to do with dragons, so Spit and Peter wandered in the opposite direction leaving Biffy and Popple together.

"Spit, I don't understand how it is that McMuran didn't force you to bond with him! I know why it didn't work for Popple, it's because her full name is Popsicle and he didn't know that."

"Petersmith, the reason is that he didn't know my full name either and it has been very remiss of me not to tell it to you. Spit is my shortened name – my full name is Spitfire!"

"Oh, what a fantastic name for you, Spit. It suits you completely, particularly now that you can breathe fire!"

Spit nodded proudly, "Thank you Petersmith!" Then he started to bounce on his feet and Peter braced himself for the rough and tumble which usually followed.

They played in the dust for quite a while and only stopped every now and then Spit would launch himself into the air and fly down into the depths of the sea to catch fish. He would place each one he caught gently in front of Effel and she scoffed them up. They all knew she needed every bit of sustenance she could get if she was to fly Biffy back to Harris. Archie hung around to gobble up the stray bits that flew out of her mouth littering the ground about her.

"Now, I know why you seemed to be talking to a crow on the beach the other day Dragon boy!"

"Yes, it probably looked a bit weird at the time, but Archie understands everything. He can't answer back though. But Biffy..." Biffy looked at him enquiringly with his head on the side, "You must be a Dragon boy now as well!"

"Ha! Ha! Very funny Dragon boy!"

"It's true though. Now you have met the dragons you have to believe in them."

* * *

It wasn't long before they had to return to the cottage. It was Peter's tummy rumbling which made them all realise it was time. At least McDragon and Effel had promised to bring the boys again the following morning before they started their long drive home, so that was something to look forward to.

CHAPTER TWENTY FIVE

Their meal on the final evening was prepared and cooked totally by Biffy, under supervision. He had happily peeled potatoes and the neeps, otherwise called swede, for their dinner. He wrapped the haggis they had bought in Stornoway in foil and put it in a water bath in the oven to cook. Then he mashed the potato adding lots of butter and some warm milk to it, doing the same but, without the milk, to the swede.

"Well done Biffy!" Peter's dad told him. "You did that all on your own. Perhaps you're going to be a chef when you get older."

Biffy looked rather proud, he wasn't used to praise.

* * *

It was two very quiet boys who sat in the back of the car on the way home. Peter hated to be parted from the dragons although he knew he could talk to Spit at any time he wanted. Biffy on the other hand was very sad. He was going back to a home life which was not at all happy and Peter just wished that they could do something about it. He'd talked to McDragon about it on their last flight home and McDragon said he had discussed a plan of sorts with the other dragons, although they did not totally understand the problem. He explained what they had decided to Peter, who was keen to try it out. He didn't say a word about it to Biffy though.

"Dad, will we be coming here again soon?"

"I think so Peter. I have a lot of work to do which involves Harris, and the isle of Lewis too, so I'll need to return. Seeing as you like it so much I'll try and time it to fit in with school holidays."

"That'd be great! Do you think Biffy could come as well when we come back?"

"I'll talk to your mum about it. It might mean you have to share your room."

"I don't mind, would you Biffy?"

Biffy sighed in amazement, he was absolutely thrilled at the thought of being able to return to such a magical place. He'd never even dreamed that he might be invited to join them again, bearing in mind that he had been a stowaway in the first place.

"I would so love to come again! That would be so amazing! Thank you!" and he beamed from ear to ear in delight, he had something to look forward to, so life wouldn't be quite as miserable as before.

"In that case, I'll talk to your parents about it Biffy. You know you're going to be in trouble for running away and hiding in the car?"

"Yes sir, I realise that," he looked rather downcast at the thought.

"I'll do my best to make sure that your father doesn't make your punishment a physical one."

"Thank you, sir! Thank you for showing me how to cook as well, I think I might try to do some more at home. That'll make it a bit easier for my mum."

"You seem to have a knack for it, Biffy." Biffy beamed at this.

Peter chatted to Spit on and off, talking in his head rather than out loud. Spit was enjoying himself practising his flying as often as he could to try and make his wings stronger. He really wanted to be able to fly to the seers' cave to see if it gave some idea of where he came from, but he was determined that his best friend, Petersmith, had to be there with him.

"Maybe next time I'm on the Isle of Harris we can do that." Peter encouraged him.

* * *

On arrival in their home town Peter's dad drove straight over to Biffy's house. It was the weekend so Biffy's parents were both at home. Peter was told to stay in the car and Peter's dad went with Biffy so that he could speak to the parents. When his dad got back in the car he looked rather fierce as he said.

"A strange man is that one but don't tell Biffy I said that!"

"I won't dad. Did you manage to make it alright for Biffy?"

"I certainly hope so. I told him that Biffy wouldn't run off again like that and how much we had enjoyed having him with us. His dad looked very surprised at that… I don't think he spends much time with the lad."

It was good seeing his mum and Alice again. Alice was quite amazed that Peter had got on with Biffy and even more so when he asked his mum if perhaps she could sometimes give Biffy some cooking lessons when she had time.

* * *

Back at school Peter and Biffy agreed they would start meeting up to walk there together each day. They had lots to chat about and, naturally, it nearly always involved dragons.

The following Saturday Peter made a surprise visit to Biffy's house. He walked up the path and knocked loudly on the front door. Biffy's mum opened the door a little way and Peter was sad to see that she had a big bruise on her arm.

"Can I come in for a moment to see Biffy please?" he asked politely.

She very hesitantly let him through the door and he could hear Biffy's dad calling out to find out who it was.

"It's that boy, Peter, to see Biffy, that's all!"

She showed Peter into the sitting room and went to call Biffy. Biffy's dad was ensconced in a big armchair, a newspaper on his lap and a can of beer balanced on the arm of the chair. His nose and cheeks were a bit pink so Peter guessed he'd had more than one can.

As Peter heard Biffy coming down the stairs he gripped the two dragon scales that he had in his pockets making sure he held each one firmly, one in each hand just as he'd been instructed. He felt the tingle up the back of his neck. Just as Biffy's dad brought the can up to his lips, Peter muttered very quietly, "Now!" and then there was a flash, not as big as the one that Spit had loosed on Biffy and his gang all that time ago but something softer. It looked a bit like a magical arrow which, with a dragon's roar, shot across the room to bat Biffy's dad on the forehead. He collapsed backwards and his eyes closed.

"What have you done, Dragon boy?"

"Just wait, Biffy. You'll see."

A loud snore reverberated throughout the room.

They waited quietly together. Biffy's mum was in the kitchen clattering china as she washed up and apart from the snoring there was no other sound. Rhonda, Biffy's sister, must have been out or in her bedroom.

Eyelids twitched and then Biffy's dad shook himself awake looking rather confused. "What happened then? I seem to have nodded off! Very strange." His hand automatically clasped the can of beer and he raised it to his mouth.

"Ergg! That tastes nasty – it must be off. Get me another Biffy!" No please of course.

Biffy ran out of the room and fetched another couple of cans in. His dad popped one open and poured it straight into his mouth and spluttered, "Horrid! Something wrong with that!"

He tugged at the ring pull on the next can and it hissed as it opened.

"Don't like that at all, it tastes off! I think I'll go to the pub instead." With that he left the room and they heard the front door bang behind him.

"Let's go for a walk Biffy."

153

"OK. Mum! I'm just going out with Peter, I won't be long! Dad's gone off to the pub."

They walked down the road and sat down on a bench at the edge of a small green which overlooked the pub. It wasn't long at all before Biffy's dad appeared again. The expression on his face was very strange and rather subdued and he kept looking back at the pub.

"What happened then Dragon boy?"

Without saying a word Peter held out Seraphina's dragon scale and Biffy took hold of one side of it. Peter also clasped Spit's scale so he could hear everything that would pass between the big dragon and Biffy.

"Biffy! With Petersmith's help, we dragons thought long and hard of a gift so we could thank you for your bravery. Dragon magic can do amazing things and you will find that your father should have changed a little. Beer should now be something he doesn't like the taste of, not that we dragons have ever had any. Petersmith seemed to believe that this might be part of the cause of your problems at home. It may also alter his thinking in more subtle ways, but only time will tell that. We do hope you like your present. Dragon magic is something very special and should not usually be used that way but this was quite definitely an exception and very well deserved. We look forward to seeing you both again very soon!"

Biffy almost fell off the bench in amazement!

He shouted, "Thank you! Thank you so very much!"

"Our pleasure, Master Biffy!"

Peter's grip on Spit's scale loosened as he said, "Over and out, Spit! Speak to you soon!"

What a fabulous end to their adventure!

NOTE FROM THE AUTHOR

I hope you enjoyed reading "Effel" and if you have time please could you put a review on Amazon about it. A good review encourages other readers to try it.

Do turn the page to read the first chapters of the third book in the "McDragon" series which is called "Finnia".

Finnia
The Third Book in the McDragon Series

CHAPTER ONE

Dragon magic flickered around the cave up high in the snow-capped mountains. The dragon could sense the arrival of a strange boy and she snorted fire which lit up the stone walls surrounding her.

* * *

The rain was sheeting down onto their heads as they trudged along the footpath to where they were staying. Their anoraks were doing a great job of repelling the rain but their trousers were soaked through from the top of their boots up to the edge of their coats.

"What do you think of this weather then Dragon boy?"

"Good weather for ducks is what my dad would say!" was Peter's answer to his friend Biffy.

They were on yet another school trip. It was early spring and the powers that be had decided that the north of Wales was a good place for their geography field trip where they could stay in a small hostel on the edge of a hamlet. Beautiful high mountains with white tops edged the skyline around them.

As they got closer to the hostel Peter felt a tiny warning prickle at the back of his neck, he turned to see whether Biffy had felt it as well.

"That was odd, wasn't it Dragon boy?"

"It affected you too? It felt like magic to me."

"Hmm," was the short answer. Biffy was beginning to look a bit red and was puffing with the effort of the trek to the house. He was quite a chubby chap compared to his small skinny friend. He rather liked his food and since he'd stowed away in Peter's dad's car when Peter and his dad were on a trip to the Isle of Harris he'd developed a passion for cooking, which didn't help his waistline at all.

The tingling feeling had passed, much to Peter's relief, but he wondered what on earth had caused it. He could hear the other boys who were with them chatting aimlessly around them indicating that the magic had not touched them in any way at all.

The panting next to him was getting louder and Peter found himself slowing his pace down so that the two of them could continue to walk together.

When they eventually stepped through the door of the hostel Peter looked around him. It was quite basic, but at least they weren't in a tent this time. Mr Trubshaw, the geography teacher who was leading their party, quickly organised them into different rooms. Peter and Biffy were in a room with four other boys and the two lads immediately made a dash for two beds next to one another by the tall window. Not that anyone else wanted to be near them or would even consider fighting them for the best beds in the room. Biffy used to be the class bully and he and his gang had tormented Peter mercilessly over quite a long period of time until, Spit, Peter's young dragon friend, had blasted Biffy with dragon magic. Although Biffy had mellowed considerably over the last few months the other children had, understandably, long memories.

They'd been told to hang their wet coats up in the bathroom on pegs which were lined up over a big old fashioned bulky radiator.

When Peter changed into his dry trousers he made sure he transferred his two dragon scales from the pocket of his damp jeans – he couldn't take any risks about losing them, they were what he used to chat to Spit, who lived in Scotland. All he had to do was to hold on to Spit's scale tightly and think of the little dragon and lo and behold they could see one another in their heads and chat as if on the telephone. Peter also had a second, bigger dragon scale, which belonged to the big dragoness, Seraphina, and that worked the same way. Not that he talked to her the way he did Spit – that scale was really for emergencies only.

Biffy nodded when he saw what Peter was doing, he too could speak to the dragons through the scales, but they had been given to Peter because he was the one who was deemed dragon kin by the dragons.

"Keep them safe, whatever you do, Peter!"

"Too right – I wouldn't want anyone else to get hold of them!"

Biffy had the grace to look a little guilty because

when they'd been on the last school trip to Scotland he'd "borrowed" the smaller scale to try and understand what it was.

Peter rubbed the back of his neck again, "There's that feeling again!" he muttered to Biffy, "Can you feel it?"

"Yeah, I can. What do you think it means?"

"I guess we'll find out in time, but as I'm not touching the dragon scales it can't be to do with them."

"Let's go and find something to eat, I'm starving!" No surprises there.

CHAPTER TWO

The afternoon snack was quite filling, sandwiches and cake and Biffy was very happy to hear that they would be having supper later as well. He chattered on and on to Peter about it, guessing what they might be having.

"Shame it's not going to be mussels with spaghetti like your dad cooks! Or haggis and neeps. I bet it's something like sausages and beans!"

"Well I happen to like bangers and mash."

"But you also like mussels or that nice mackerel we caught when we went fishing. That was lovely! Did I tell you that last week your mum showed me how to make lasagne and I'm going to try to do that when we get home?"

"How come you are always thinking of your stomach?"

"There's nothing wrong with liking my food. I might be a chef when I am older, I can't see me working in an office somehow."

Peter just smiled. Biffy's talent for cooking was growing fast and he'd really got the hang of making cakes.

"I wonder what cakes they make here in Wales? It

might be nice to learn how to make something that is traditionally Welsh."

The sun seemed to be peaking through the grey clouds and the rain had finally ceased as Mr Trubshaw told the boys that they could have the rest of the afternoon off and either explore or they could read in their rooms if they preferred but, tomorrow would be the start of the school work he added ominously.

Peter and Biffy decided to take the outdoors option. Biffy thought they might be able to see if there was a baker's shop so he could get an idea for different cakes and pies. Peter didn't like to tell him that it was rather late in the afternoon for bakers to have much on display, but he wanted to be in the open air so was happy to walk with Biffy down what passed as the high road.

The radiator had done its job and their coats and trousers were nicely dry. Biffy continued chuntering on about food as they walked through the village. It seemed that there was only one shop, and when Biffy peered through the window he was quite excited to see that at the back of it there were racks which must normally hold bread and cakes and various other goodies.

Peter wasn't that bothered so stared across to look at the high crags in the distance. Was he imagining it or could he see something circling the peaks? He patted his pockets but his binoculars must be in his bag. Drat! The back of his neck prickled.

The shop owner gave them a cheerful smile and came to the door when he saw Biffy staring in through the window to ask if there was anything he could help them with.

Biffy jumped straight in wanting to know about local

delicacies and whether they were made on the premises. Mr Rees seemed quite thrilled to find someone who was interested and told him that if he cared to get up at 5.00 a.m. in the morning he could come down and see what they were baking when he made bread, pies and cakes which were delivered to other villages in their van. He did add that Biffy had to get permission of the teacher.

"Just come through the side passage to the back door and knock. I'll hear you and let you in."

"Thank you! I'd love to do that!"

The boys ambled on their way.

"You'll have to go on your own to the shop, I don't fancy doing that, but I may get up early just to explore a bit on my own."

"OK, so long as you don't stray too far. Dragon kin you may be but you still need to be careful."

Peter looked back at the mountains but whatever it was had disappeared.

They followed a small footpath which seemed to run along the back of the village. Biffy was soon puffing and out of breath again as it was quite a steep walk up the hill and eventually he sat down on a boulder at the edge of the path saying he would wait there while Peter carried on. As a matter of fact, that suited Peter fine because before Biffy had become his best friend he had been used to being on his own, so he carried on for a while. Eventually, after a quick look at his watch he decided he'd better get back to Biffy who wouldn't want to be late for supper.

It was two tired boys who finally put their heads down on their pillows and fell asleep immediately. It had been a very long day.

To see when "Finnia" is available follow me on my facebook page: Pamghoward@pamghowardchildrensbooks or twitter: Pam Howard@pamghoward

Or my website is:
https://www.pamghowardchildrensbooks.com

* * *

I have also published another book called "Spangle" and I have included a chapter of this so that you can take a look at it. If you like it, then it's available from amazon.co.uk

Spangle

CHAPTER ONE

"Spangle is a funny word," Mabel thought as she watched a little robin manfully having a tug of war with a worm that seemed far bigger than himself and which appeared to be getting longer and longer.

The gravestone that she was resting on was cold on her back as she sat beside the freshly covered grave, tears trickling down her cheeks. She'd placed the single yellow daffodil with its long green stem across the middle of the mounded clods of earth, the yellow head pointing towards the small wooden cross which had the name "Daffodil" on it. As she sat there she thought she felt the lightest touch on her shoulder and the smell of lavender and roses wafted gently around her.

"What am I going to do?" she muttered feebly. "I miss you so much!"

She remembered the distant look that had come into her Aunt's eyes and how she had spoken in a dreamy voice a few months before she had died.

"When the time comes you will need to find a dragon's head and you must not go alone. I do not know how this will come about but the code word is "Spangle." Remember that, "Spangle" and remember the robin too!" Mabel had repeated those words until they were etched into her brain and her Aunt seemed to doze off after that. When she woke up a little while later her Aunt had sat up straight and looked around herself, mystified.

"What were we talking about?" she asked.

"A dragon's head and Spangle and a robin."

Her Aunt had looked at her strangely and shook her head.

"Really, how odd," she muttered.

"Why will I need to leave Aunt Daffodil, I'm happy here with you?"

There was silence and Mabel repeated her question.

Her Aunt shook her head again as if clearing out cobwebs and when Mabel pressed her further had had no recollection of what she had said. Now she was no more, so Mabel would never know.

More tears streamed down Mabel's cheeks and she felt the breeze brush against her hair fluffing it gently, still carrying the faint aroma of lavender and roses with it, her Aunt's smell. Mabel looked about her – strangely there were no lavender or rose bushes close by.

She glanced up at the sky and realised that she must go back to the house very soon. She couldn't call it home any more, not now that Aunt Gertrude lived there with her. Aunt Gertrude had arrived the day after Daffodil had died and insisted that she was Daffodil's relative and would look after Mabel and arrange the funeral. No-one seemed to question that, even though she didn't look at all like Aunt Daffodil, more like a squat warty toad and what's more she smelled like a toad, very slimy. Mabel didn't like her at all but there was no-one else to go to. Her eyes were always drawn to the large growth on the side of her chin – it had one lone dark hair growing out of it which wobbled when Aunt Gertrude moved her head. Yuck! It made Mabel shiver just to think of her.

The robin hopped about near her feet tipping its head from side to side watching her the whole time. He tweeted a pretty little song and looked so pleased with himself it made her smile for a brief moment.

She moved very slowly to her feet realising that she couldn't put it off any longer and trudged reluctantly back to the house. The back gate into the rear garden banged against the post as she let herself through it and then walked quietly down the side of the house. She stopped near an open window as she could hear voices.

"So you've agreed a figure for the payment of the child? When will he pick her up?"

"I told him that I had to have cash and he's going to come tomorrow morning as he has insisted on taking a look at the merchandise first to check she is what his purchaser wants. He will return with transport and the money the following day. I'd best make sure she is clean and tidy and on her best behaviour!"

The unknown man with Gertrude snorted in amusement. "As if she would do anything other than what you told her, just like all the others. You must be quite rich by now! Anyway I'm off to see a man about a dog! I'll be back after lunch just in case you need any help."

Mabel froze against the downpipe she was standing next to, shocked. Were they talking about her? They must be because she was the only child in the house. She watched the man as he whistled tunelessly on his way down the front path and out onto the pavement. He was a big man with dirty blond hair. She couldn't see his face, but she could smell something which wasn't nice and it reminded her of dog poo when it was stuck on a shoe.

When she heard the clink of cups being dropped into the sink in the kitchen she made sure the man was out of sight before running back towards the cemetery – for some reason she felt safe there and close to her Aunt. Panting, she threw herself down by the grave sobbing loudly, her small shoulders shaking.

"Aunt Daffodil, what am I to do? Who is this man who I am being sold to? Where did I come from to end up with you? You never told me. Oh, what should I do? I have no-one!" she wailed, but quietly as she did not want anyone else to hear her and ask what was wrong. "I should leave to find this dragon's head, but I promised you I would not go without a guide and anyway I have no idea where or what the dragon's head is!"

The gentle sun beat in the sky and warmed her back as gradually she became more in control of herself and aware of her surroundings. She heard the crunch of gravel and someone moving along the churchyard path. Whoever it was, they were humming to themselves. She hastily wiped her tear stained face with her sleeve and sat up. The footsteps stopped beside her and when she looked up she saw a person she had never seen before. A smallish man with a beaming smile looked down at her where she kneeled. He had a kind face with bright blue eyes and wild looking brown hair poking out from under his flat cap. He was dressed most outlandishly in a brightly coloured suit with trousers that were almost baggy and a large jacket. The colours were like a rainbow but randomly splashed across the stripes of the suit which reminded her of a clown's clothes. A robin was perched on his shoulder.

"I believe you require my services young lady," said a quietly spoken gentle voice.

"Pardon sir?"

"I believe you need my help – I am Spangle. Your Aunt Daffodil told you about me."

Mabel's mouth opened wide but no words would come out. She looked up at him – his eyes seemed to have changed colour to one green and one black.

She felt a soft breeze brush her shoulders almost giving her a hug and words seemed to whisper in the air around her smelling of lavender and roses, "Remember what I told you."

"Mr err Spangle, how can you help me?"

"I will be your guide to help you find the dragon's head, but I have had to come sooner than expected because I hear your so-called Aunt Gertrude has other plans for you!" The robin flew from his shoulder and landed on Mabel, tweeting into her ear.

"How could you know, I only overheard her talking just a short while ago?"

"Let's just say I have my means," he said mysteriously. "Now we must make a plan, but we need to move very quickly as we only have a short while to get you away. It could be a long and strange route to the dragon's head and I am not sure of the way but it will reveal itself to us as we go. We will probably be followed by Gertrude's so-called brother. He is a Snifter, so we must hide our tracks as best we can. Snifters are generally very good scouts, they sniff out their prey. Let me think." And with that the brightly clothed man called Mr Spangle sat down in a cross legged position next to her and pulled a small flute-like tube out of his pocket which he put against his lips and blew. The music wafted around them, bright and happy and Mabel felt herself relax. The robin hopped down onto the ground near Mr Spangle and twittered beside him, eventually ending up on his shoulder again. It looked very much like the same one that had been with her earlier.

After a while he stopped playing and looked deep into her eyes. Strange, she thought, his eyes have changed colour again.

"You have to trust me," he said. "I know you should not go off with strangers but Daffodil told you that the code word would be Spangle, and Spangle I am, and the robin is here as well. Tonight you need to decide what clothes you should bring with you. Do you have a backpack?"

"Yes, we bought one when I went to Brownie camp."

"Get that out and put some clothes into it. You will need some warm jumpers and socks. Pack some trainers but when it is time to leave wear your wellies and thick socks and a good rainproof coat. You must not take too much or it will be too heavy to carry. Hide everything in a safe place in your room and I'll meet you here tomorrow at this time so we can decide when to leave on our quest. Be brave, I know you can! Remember you are not alone anymore."

He put the flute away, stood up and took off his grey

flat cap, which was at odds with his spangle coloured suit, and bowed.

"By the way, you have mud on your nose," he said with a big grin on his face, and then he waved as he went back the way he had come, the robin still on his shoulder. She could hear him humming.

Mabel realised she hadn't said much at all and although she hadn't actually agreed to meet him tomorrow, she knew that she would. What other option did she have? If she didn't go she could end up anywhere. He must be her guide because she hadn't mentioned the name, Spangle, or the robin to anyone else.

That night, after a tea of beans on toast yet again, except this time the bread that was toasted was going a little green at the edges, when Mabel went to her room she pulled the backpack down from the top of the wardrobe. Then she started to think about what she should take with her.

"Clean pants, vest and socks for sure, and pyjamas," she muttered. "Spare jeans and if I wear two jumpers that will save some room in the bag." She pushed her trainers down to the bottom of the bag, followed by the underwear. There was one good thing about Aunt Gertrude, she had no idea what clothes Mabel had. Last, but by no means least, she pushed the favourite teddy that Aunt Daffodil had given her into one of the side pockets with his head poking over the flap. A small notepad and pencil also went in. She tested the weight of the bag – not too bad. She shoved the backpack into the bottom of the wardrobe and flung a coat over it to hide it. Then she curled up in bed and before she knew it was sound asleep. It had been an exhausting and emotional day.

Please see my website:

https://pamghowardchildrensbooks.com for further details.

As mentioned before, if you have time to put a review for "Effel" on either the Amazon website or troubador.co.uk website that would be amazing thank you!